"Let's be direct. ... bust my balls," Sean murmured

Fiona reached out with both hands, gripping the ends of his undone tie—that and his rolled-up sleeves evidence of a hard-knock day—and pulled down gently. A hitched breath separated their faces, their mouths, the singe of her lipstick.

"Bust your balls? Oh, no, sir." She laughed softly. "I'll be more gentle than that."

Her hands floated downward, one knuckle brushing against the awakening bulge in his pants. Or maybe she hadn't touched him at all and he was just wishing she had.

At any rate, Fiona stepped away from him, tugging at her short sexy skirt. Then she took a stand, hands on hips, a challenge in her raised eyebrows.

A player. Fiona Cruz was obviously one of those teases in a suit, someone who flaunted her femininity around the boys' locker room, working them with a come-hither/hands-off strategy. Controlling.

The female version of *him*.

There was one way to handle the Fionas of the world, Sean knew. Get down to business first....

Then make sure they burned up the bedsheets together—big-time.

Dear Reader,

Can a woman enjoy a physical relationship without becoming territorial or possessive? That's what my hero and heroine are about to find out. See, Sean and Fiona have made a bet with each other that she won't become attached to him during their steamy, one-month affair, and the winner gets an all-expense-paid vacation to a Caribbean island. Not a bad situation in any case, I think.

Sound fun? I definitely thought so. These playmates are full of wit and charm, and whenever they were together, I couldn't help having a good time. They were fun to listen to and behind closed doors...my, oh, my. These fireballs couldn't keep their hands off each other. Writing my first Blaze was a golden opportunity to go where I'd never gone before—and it was a blast!

I hope you enjoy meeting Sean and Fiona as much as I enjoyed writing about them. In the meantime, please check out my Web site at www.crystal-green.com.

Playtime is about to begin...

Crystal Green

Books by Crystal Green

SILHOUETTE SPECIAL EDITION

SILHOUETTE SINGLE TITLE

*Kane's Crossing
**Montana Mavericks

PLAYMATES

Crystal Green

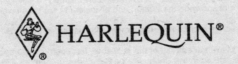

HARLEQUIN®

TORONTO • NEW YORK • LONDON
AMSTERDAM • PARIS • SYDNEY • HAMBURG
STOCKHOLM • ATHENS • TOKYO • MILAN • MADRID
PRAGUE • WARSAW • BUDAPEST • AUCKLAND

To Lulu and Scott Shields.
Thanks for your knowledge, guidance
and love of a good time!

ISBN 0-373-79125-9

PLAYMATES

Copyright © 2004 by Chris Marie Green.

1

WHEN SEAN MCINTYRE first saw her, his sex drive let out an endless, shuddering wolf whistle. One that would've brought down the high-rise building if Los Angeles hadn't been so strict about fortifying the place against occasional earthquakes.

Or another natural disaster trigger like his new co-worker.

He settled back in his leather office chair, just taking in the show, a grin easing over his mouth as she leaned against the door frame. All long legs, curves and cat-nip.

Dark gypsy hair waved softly past her shoulders, matching the black smoke of her eyes. She aimed a lowered gaze at him, the tips of her red lips swooping upward in a gesture more suited to a wet dream than the business offices of Stellar Public Relations, Incorporated.

Sean raised an eyebrow, amused. Intrigued.

But, as usual, Louis Martin screwed up the moment, bursting past the woman in a flutter of kinetic overload.

"There she is. Didn't know where you disappeared

to,'' said the short, balding boss man. ''One second I'm giving you the tour, the next you're...''

The woman interrupted him with one sultry glance. Louis almost fell backward from the force of it.

''Sorry,'' she said, her voice as thick and slow as honey dripping from a fingertip. She nodded toward the window while returning her gaze to Sean. ''I prefer the view in this office.''

He bit back a laugh. Cheeky. Already he liked her. Already he wanted to peel off that slightly see-through, butterfly-sleeved red suit that pushed the limits of professional wear. Sharp, flashy, powerful. All the things a PR representative should be.

And then some.

Louis fidgeted with his tie. ''The view. Right. Your office'll be down the hall though.''

Time to open his mouth, Sean supposed. ''This is my lion's den. Not fit for a lady.''

''No wonder I feel right at home.'' She flashed him that cool/hot gaze again.

Sean shifted. Nice. A thirty-two-year-old schoolboy with a hard-on. Should he grab a textbook and hide behind it while he got to his feet to shake hands? No English Lit or Trig tomes available, you say? Then maybe he could just stay seated and zoom his wheeled office chair on over to her, introducing himself as half the cad he actually was.

That's right. A gentleman would stand up, take a woman's hand, pay her proper respect. But gentlemen probably refrained from popping wood the second a beautiful female came within range.

He flicked a manila folder off the desk to his lap—
the better to fool you with, my dear—and performed
the chair slide.

But his cautious move didn't throw her off, not if
that knowing gleam in her eyes was any indication.

What the hell, thought Sean. He grinned as he stood,
flipping aside the folder, extending his hand. "Sean
McIntyre."

The woman perused his outstretched palm, her gaze
slipping to the front of his pants, her mouth still heated
by that lazy grin. She knew he was turned on. Not that
it made her a genius.

She tucked her fingers into his hand, sliding a nail
along his thumb in a wickedly disguised shake.
"Fiona Cruz. Pleased to meet you."

Cruz. The name rang an alarm. He'd heard of her
successes as a marketing machine for actors. She was
good. Damned good. But hadn't there been some hint
of scandal surrounding her…?

Time seemed to furl around itself as their skin
pulsed with the contact, touches languishing, almost
as if both of them wanted to see who would let go
first.

Louis's voice sawed apart their grip, but not their
sustained eye contact.

"We brought on Fiona because she's gangbusters."

Sean coolly acknowledged the weasel's remark.
This introduction was Louis's way of turning on the
burner under Sean's chair, wasn't it?

"Got that covered, Martie," he said, knowing the
nickname would piss off the other guy.

The boss man's cheeks reddened. "It's Louis. As in Martin."

Fiona Cruz had started to wander around Sean's office, trailing her hand over the rigid, metal bookshelves, the writhing steel sculpture in the corner. A flame in the center of a frozen twist of furniture.

He couldn't help admiring her beautiful ass, wanting to cup the curves of it, rocking her against his groin, feeling every voluptuous inch of her opening for him....

"McIntyre?"

Louis again.

"What?"

"Fiona's brought her rising star with her to the firm. Lincoln Castle."

Sean blanched. "The soap star? *That* Lincoln Castle?"

As Fiona stopped by the window, which overlooked Wilshire Boulevard with its palm trees and summer-in-the-city streets, she tossed her words over a shoulder. "There's only one man with a name that... singular."

Rage kicked him into gear, forcing his footsteps over to Louis, where he shadowed the boss with his height. "Look, do you have any idea how Castle is connected to my new client?"

Louis shrugged. "Of course. Say, McIntyre, I've got a conference call with Edgar Lux and his publishing house. Can you show Fiona to her office when she's ready?" Then he lowered his voice. "That is, unless she gets comfortable in *your* chair."

Rather than saying something that would cause Louis to fly into a fit, Sean kept his mouth shut, electing instead to usher his boss from the room with a thanks-a-lot glare.

Louis dashed away, leaving Sean alone with a woman who could very well be the end of his career at Stellar. If you could call it a career anymore.

He turned his attention to Fiona, trying to focus his anger. But he was distracted by the way her dress caught the sun through its sheer material, a dreamcatcher winding darker hopes through the threads of red while allowing fantasies to pass through.

"Let me guess," she said, her back still to him, "watch out for Louis Martin."

"The guy's harmless, unless you don't know how to play office politics."

She turned around with a smile, leaning against the window frame, shifting the sunlight and blinding him with another jab of pure lust.

"I know how to play," she said. "Do you?"

He couldn't hold back a sardonic laugh. Another sweeping gaze over that jazz-baby body. "Listen, Ms. Cruz—"

"Call me Fiona."

"Fiona." The purr of her name caught in his throat. A professional-suicide hairball.

To compensate, he sauntered nearer to her, hovering. Her chin lifted as she stood her ground, tension snapping between their bodies while he leaned in close enough to catch her scent. A tang of fruit—fresh, exotic.

"Let's be direct. You're here to bust my balls," he murmured.

She reached out with both hands, gripping the ends of his undone tie—that and his rolled-up sleeves evidence of a hard-knock day—and pulled down gently. A hitched breath separated their faces, their mouths.

"Bust your balls? Oh, no, sir." She laughed softly. "I'll be more gentle than that."

Her hands floated downward, one knuckle brushing against the reawakening bulge in his pants. Or maybe she hadn't touched him at all and he was just wishing she had.

At any rate, she stepped away from him, shoulder sliding against his arm with lackadaisical disregard. Then she took a stand, hands on hips, a challenge in her raised eyebrows.

A player. Fiona Cruz was obviously one of those teases in a suit, one who flaunted her femininity around the boys' locker room, working them with a come-hither/hands-off strategy. Controlling.

The female version of him.

There was one way to handle the Fionas of the world. Get down to business first, then... What would she do if he took her up on those silent, raw-edged invitations?

He leaned against the back of a leather couch, folded his arms over his chest. "You came fully loaded to Stellar, didn't you? Lincoln Castle, the Brad Pitt of daytime soaps."

"He's a good friend. We've known each other since college. Besides, I excel at what I do."

"You'll need to. His star's not so golden anymore. And he was going places, too, with that Aaron Spelling gig he used to have."

There. A flinch. A different tilt of the hip. And, damn her, even though she wasn't smiling anymore, her lips still tipped up at the ends, giving her an I-know-something-you-don't-know upper hand.

"Linc missed daytime acting, and *Flamingo Beach* made an offer he couldn't refuse," Fiona said.

"Yeah," Sean replied, "he's so thrilled to be back on a soap that he's hired his own private publicist."

She acknowledged his point by staying cool and silent. Many soap actors made good use of the PR rep the soap employed—unless they decided to go "big time."

Finally, after a sufficiently maddening pause, she responded. "Lincoln's always been in demand, but he wants the security of being in a soap right now. That's all."

"Good try, Dr. Spin." He almost mentioned the actor's rumored time in rehab, and how no one outside the soaps—where Lincoln had a strong fan base— would probably ever take a chance on him. But he didn't say a word.

Sean could relate to Castle, because he knew a lot about seeing your professional star fall from the highest point, knew a lot about battling one unworkable PR disaster after another: rising stars who enjoyed "working girls," fading actresses who climbed on political soap boxes and aired extremely conservative opinions. Sean McIntyre, as good as he was, couldn't save every reputation.

But he'd get back on top, especially with his new account.

He continued. ''You know I handle Lakota Lang's publicity now?''

''Ah.'' Fiona was grinning again.

''I can't believe Louis didn't sense a conflict of interest.''

''Why, because Lakota and Linc once slept together?''

''*Once* slept together?'' Sean chuffed. ''They burned the sheets from coast to coast. In several very public positions, too.''

''I know. Passion.'' Fiona's gaze drifted to the ceiling, all Cinderella soap dreams and glass slippers. But as quick as the pop of a bubble, the soft sparkle in her eyes disappeared. Right back to the career woman. ''Isn't it convenient that they're on the same show again? Imagine the publicity we could work, the possibilities.''

''For what? Them killing each other?'' Sean shook his head. ''This is trouble waiting to happen, and you're having delusions of grandeur.''

''Pshaw.'' Fiona moved to his desk, sat on the edge of it, rankling Sean with the territorial gesture. ''You need to look at the bright side, Mac. We've got a gold mine.''

Mac? ''So we're pals already,'' he said dryly.

''Hey, you scratch my back, I'll scratch yours.''

A hunger stretched in his belly, pawing at the inside of his skin.

He grinned. "Does the offer extend to—"

"—Bad boy." She wagged her finger at him. "We're talking business."

"You do *business* with all the shy delicacy of Anna Nicole Smith."

She watched him, tracking his movements as he rose from the couch. "I can tell you're going to keep me on my toes."

Right. Either there or on her back.

That wolfish howl screamed through his veins once again.

Jerk.

Not that he'd ever heard any complaints about his libido and its excesses. He loved women: their slippery skin after a bout of sex, their sighs of pleasure in his ear, their muscles clenching around his cock as they came. But sometimes Sean wondered if he'd be married with kids by now, happy as the families in a fast-food commercial, if it hadn't been for the way he was brought up.

Forget all that. He had business to do.

He brushed by her, trying not to let her mouth-watering perfume get the best of him, then sat in his chair. Claiming it.

Fiona scanned him over her shoulder, eyes unreadable. "I like a guy who can give me a run for my money. We're going to be quite a team."

"I work alone."

She stood, started to leave. "That's not what I heard."

"You've done your research with me, huh?" He laughed. "I guess I won't make the mistake of underestimating you."

She turned around, holding up a finger. "That's right. And the same goes for me. I know you're tops. Three years ago, you engineered the Yum Gum blitz campaign winning the Guerilla Marketers of the Year award from *Brandweek* magazine. Not bad. Not bad at all."

Sean wasn't fool enough to swell with pride. Three years was a long time. Time enough to lose your footing.

"Oh, before I leave you in peace," she added, "that children's charity event you have Lakota attending tomorrow night? Linc's going, too. He's got a big heart and wants to help raise money."

"Is his heart as big as his ambition?"

He wanted to know the same about her, too. Not that heart mattered much in this business.

Fiona lifted her hands in a gracefully dramatic gesture. "I've sent out press releases hinting that Linc's an all-around enormous man. Not that I've seen anything firsthand."

Cheeky. "Uh-huh, right, you're college friends. FYI, Lakota Lang's a micromanaging superstar in the making, and that means she wants me at the event to oversee her moment in the spotlight."

"I'm sure she'll be more comfortable flying solo once she gets used to her diva role." Was that a proxy swipe at his client, establishing the ill will between Lakota and Lincoln?

Sean's voice took on an edge of sarcasm. "All the same, I'll report back to you, boss."

"No need. I'll be there. Linc's escorting me. More social than business, but I'll be wearing my professional demeanor."

Friends, huh? A claw of jealousy scored Sean, but he ignored it. Sure, he'd love to see what Fiona Cruz was made of when she stepped *out* of the office, but the fulfillment of his curiosity might blow his career to smithereens.

"Great," he said, pausing when she didn't move completely out of his domain. "Need me to show you to your dungeon?"

"No." She took pains to adjust her sleeves, the filmy material breezing over her dusky skin. "I already know where it is. Remember, I've done my research, Mac."

And, without further ado, she left him sitting behind the desk, his emerging grin beating back a more prudent frown.

Sure, he was hungry for more, but that didn't mean he was happy about it.

THE NEXT NIGHT, at the fund-raiser in the Renaissance Hollywood Hotel, Lincoln Castle was reluctant to come out of the men's rest room.

So, naturally, Fiona went in.

"Linc?" She poked her head around the door.

Two men stood before the urinal, mouths agape.

One zipped up and deserted the room, shooting Fiona a dirty glare, which she answered with her best charmingly apologetic smile. The other man took his time, nodding at her and leering.

She ignored him, slipping farther into the forbidden space. "Linc, I know you're in here."

"Stage fright." His words echoed off the tile. "I'll get over it."

Fiona's nerves jumped in sympathy for her friend. He was fine in front of the cameras, but live audiences? Another beast all together.

She followed his voice to a stall. The door creaked open to reveal her college pal. Lincoln Castle—a stage name for Kevin Lincoln. He was a composite of every heartthrob-boat cliché imaginable, with a six-foot tall, freestyle-weight physique, tanned skin, blond hair and blue eyes. All of that in a tux, besides.

"Hey," she said.

He looked so lost and pathetic propped up by the wall, eyes closed. "Just waiting for the Alka-Seltzer to take hold."

"Do you think that 'plop-plop-fizz-fizz' will chase away more than your anxiety?"

Linc blinked his eyes open after the other bathroom patron slammed the door on his way out. "Thanks. I needed to be reminded of Lakota. That, coupled with this bid for comeback success, really makes my night."

Still, he managed a grin.

It was the same disarmingly sensitive gesture she'd known throughout her early twenties. Same guy, even though soap stardom, a featured role on a hot prime-time drama then a brief, mortifying obscurity had claimed him.

"See," she said, "you're better already. Let's go."

"You in some kind of rush?"

Fiona raised her brows. "Why would I be?"

Why? Could it be the fact that Sean McIntyre—Mac—would be in the Grand Ballroom?

When she focused again, Linc was assessing her.

"You're putting off steam, Fi."

"Me?" Fiona walked away, propelled by a nervous, sexual energy. She could almost feel Mac in the building, could almost hunt him down with her awakened senses.

Without warning, the bathroom door crashed against the wall. Security guard. Wonderful.

"Miss," said the tidy little uniformed man, "this ain't the ladies' john."

Linc half stumbled out of the stall, revealing himself. Fiona discreetly checked his eyes, his scent. Good. Not drunk.

The guard held up his hands. "Hey! My girlfriend used to watch you on that Thursday night show!"

Linc modestly shrugged, and Fiona's heart went out to him. Though daytime soaps were filled with solid actors, the genre was considered a step down from prime time. But Linc didn't seem to mind right now. Like most soap actors, he genuinely loved the fans, relished the contact.

As the man asked for an autograph and repeated over and over how his honey wouldn't believe this,

Fiona stood by. Linc's connection with the public was one of his strengths.

Soon, they were on their way to the fund-raiser. The festivities were being held down the boulevard from the legendary cemented hand and footprints and refurbished glamour of the Chinese Theatre. The hotel was tucked next to the Kodak Theatre, the most recent home of the Academy Awards. Dazzle and sophistication cloaked the black-tie guests.

When she and her friend walked into the Grand Ballroom arm in arm, lulled by the DJ's background-volume techno music, blinded by photo-op flashbulbs and fake silver stars hanging from the ceiling, the first person who caught her eye was Mac.

And he was worth the wait. The man shouldn't be allowed anywhere near a tuxedo. The sight was enough to make every woman in the room implode. The way he filled out the dark, suave cut of his jacket with those steel-beam shoulders, that broad chest, those hefting-the-weight-of-the-world arms…

How would the female race survive if they were all spontaneously combusting? It just didn't seem fair.

While Linc led her farther into the roar of the party, she allowed her gaze to linger on Mac a decadent moment longer. She couldn't stop herself.

Shaded blond hair, razored to just above the collar, green eyes with a sharp-shooter squint, the rakish hint of stubbled mustache and half beard surrounding a full mouth slanted in wary repose. If you took all his features and inspected them one by one—as she'd slyly done today during a firm meeting—they'd be slightly off-kilter. Especially the subtly crooked nose and the too-strong chin.

But all together....

Whoo doggie.

As Fiona and Linc moved past the summer-night decorations featuring simulated moons glinting over the sea, past the auction items and information tables, she realized Mac wasn't alone.

The vampish Lakota Lang was leeched onto him.

After refusing drinks from a passing waiter, Linc's arm stiffened as they came to a stop on the opposite side of the empty dance floor.

She squeezed his solid bicep, hopefully lending him reassurance. "Steady."

The emotion in his voice belied his polished, pretty-boy exterior. "I'm good."

Gorgeous Linc. Not like Mac, who seemed to wear that worn-and-torn attitude like it was an outlaw's faded duster, edges shredded and beaten by a run of bad luck. You had to look past the rough smirk, the creviced slant of his cheekbones to see the bruised beauty of him.

Hey, cool it with the Snow White la-de-da fantasies, she told herself. *Get your mind back on Linc. Back on business.*

Fiona patted her friend's wrist. "Ignore Lakota, just like you've been doing."

"She doesn't make it easy."

"At least you don't have scenes together."

"Yet. And who's the guy she's salivating over?"

Fiona tried not to react, to light up inside at the

mention of Mac. Instead, she playfully pulled Linc away from the dance floor, but he wouldn't budge.

"No competition. You are a demigod," she said. "I'm telling you so. All the soap magazines tell you so."

He laughed, thank goodness. "I appreciate that, but I'm in trouble when I start believing my own press."

Fiona barely heard him. What was that woman doing to Mac, rubbing her hand up and down his arm? And...was he smiling? Reacting to the way she arched her neck when she giggled?

Oh, and she supposed that her co-worker was probably making the most of his low, sexy voice. Its touch of snake-charmer trust.

Well, yesterday's flirtatious introduction had been her fault, really. She'd come on strong, immediately drawn to him as he'd assessed her from his chair, his long legs stretched out in front of him, cocky as you please. She loved a man who had the talent to banter, to tease. To tower over her until her body almost melted right into his.

He's a co-worker, a competitor, Fi. Don't forget it.

Right. Right. Her conscience was absolutely right. And her pride couldn't afford to lose another PR gig.

Even from across the room, Fiona felt his rifle-sight gaze on her before actually meeting his eyes. They hadn't said a word to each other in the office today, both consumed with arranging photo shoots, media interviews and guest appearances for other clients. But, right now, the awareness was flammable. Unavoidable.

A quaking need roared through her, tearing through

every inch of skin until it splashed into her belly, dripping into a steady pulse between her legs. God, the ache. The want.

He must have seen the desire in the angle of her body. With a devilish grin, he toasted her from across the floor. She returned a jaunty salute with her own champagne flute.

Lakota must have seen their exchange, because the redhead latched onto Mac's muscular arm, staring stilettos at Fiona.

Linc walked away, taking her with him. "More Alka-Seltzer."

Fiona tugged him back, gently, so no one would notice the tension. "Don't go drama on me. You didn't keep me on as your publicist so I could look the other way as you make a scene."

"You're my employee, Fi."

His tone was light, but she knew better. Before rehab, when Lincoln got agitated, he got into trouble. That was the problem with being talented and catered to. But she loved him enough to continue keeping him in line. He'd almost ruined his career after the breakup with Lakota, who was at the time an extra on Linc's daytime set. His broken heart had led to an excess of drinking, partying, getting into scrapes that Fiona and Linc's manager constantly got him out of.

And she cared too much to see him fall apart again.

"Listen," she said, "I appreciate how you stuck by me after I got fired at the last firm, but their lack of faith doesn't mean I don't know what I'm doing now.

Don't falter. You're going to have to put up with Lakota every day.''

She could feel his struggle in the ticking muscles of his arm, but she knew he'd pull through. She'd make sure of it.

''I can't believe she's the star of *Flamingo Beach,*'' he said, acknowledging a female fan who made it clear she recognized him by pointing and squealing. ''How the tables have turned, huh? Now *I'm* the new guy.''

Fiona flicked another gaze to Mac again, discovered that he'd left Lakota all alone, and breathed a sigh of relief. ''Don't sweat it. You'll do fine.''

He nodded, squeezed her hand. ''I suppose I will. Now if you could only keep your mind on your publicity stunts....''

She didn't have to ask what he meant. ''That man with Lakota, Sean McIntyre, works with me. There's a little flirting going on, but...''

''...But?''

Lying to Linc, to herself was useless. ''Okay, he's my kind of poison. True. But I'll be good.''

''Good? You actually know that word?'' Linc's laughter rose above the fresh set of reggae music. ''That's a new one. I thought girls with your body and appetite weren't built for flowers and valentines.''

Fiona's heart fisted, bleeding out every stupid romantic dream she hid from the world. She had no use for roses and sweet nothings anyway. Hadn't needed them for a long time, after being slammed by Ted, the ex.

Nope. Now she was in control of her life, every aspect. Her career, her family, her love…

…Or lack *of* love life.

Didn't matter. Not in the least. She got along just fine with men, keeping relationships to the essentials—sex and…well, sex. She didn't hurt anyone, they didn't hurt her. It was all fun and games, light and laughter.

No more sitting at home, crying because her man had done her wrong.

Never again.

"Fi?" said Lincoln, rubbing a hand along her bare arm. "You know *I* don't believe you're heartless."

Fiona manufactured a smile, beaming at him. "You're the only one. And you're wrong, besides."

Her friend stared at her a moment longer. He'd been there when Ted had dumped her, and she'd returned the favor with Lakota. That's what glued them together—their failures and, soon, triumphs.

"Soap hunk," she said, "there's a group of women waving you over to them. Probably for autographs and a picture or two. And I see your manager and personal assistant making a beeline for you. Escape to the fans while you can."

He straightened his bow tie, his debonair jacket, and with an amiable wink, he was off. Fiona diligently tried to keep her mind on business—damn, it was hard watching her charge like a proud mama seeing her child off to the first day of school, when Mac was somewhere around. As Linc's mini-entourage controlled the growing crowd surrounding him, he proceeded to charm the ladies, posing for photos, signing autograph books.

The night wore on, and she stayed on the outskirts of the festivities while Linc bid adieu to his fans and led the auction. He helped raise several thousand dollars for the children's charity, while a distant Lakota and other cast members from *Flamingo Beach* joined him onstage to entertain the masses.

As the presentation wound down, Fiona glanced around the ballroom, discovering that Lakota Lang was holding hands with Brendon Fillmore, a fading young James-Dean-type actor who still had enough drawing power to attract attention and probably a gossip mention in the fan magazines. Had Mac arranged their liaison, manipulating every shared laugh, every hug for the camera?

Good publicity move. But Fiona wanted to be sure Linc didn't notice. Her friend didn't need another dart to the ego.

When she checked on him, he was busy with a gaggle of adoring fans and seemingly having the time of his life. Some security guards now flanked him.

Maybe now was a good time to visit the powder room, to freshen up.

She set down her champagne and walked toward the rest room, entering a shady hall crammed with gossiping women and soap-star wannabes. Just as she spotted the ladies' room ahead, a young girl crashed into her, yelling, "I think that's Deirdre Hall! Oh. My. God." Then the fan took off, bumping Fiona into the nearest body.

A broad-shouldered, hard-chested body.

"Packed house," said a deep voice. A pair of large hands closed over her arms, steadying her, charging shock waves through the top layer of her skin.

Sucking in a breath, she looked closer, finding Mac standing over her, smiling, challenging her to pass in the limited space.

"Not much room to maneuver." She nodded her head toward the ladies' door. "Do you mind?"

He didn't move. "Go right ahead."

All right. She wouldn't be able to get by him without some full frontal contact, the jerk.

So be it. With a saucy glance, she slid her body over his. Too close. The tips of her breasts hardened and dragged against his jacket, the thin linen of his shirt, slipping over the bulk of his powerful chest, the ridges of his upper abs. At the same time, her hips swayed over his, the hitch in his crotch making her pause and hold her breath. As they stared at each other, she grew moist, achy with the possibilities.

He bent his head, his lips near her forehead, a whisper stirring her hair with warmth.

"Can't move?" he asked.

No. She wouldn't mind nestling against him for the next hour, either, his arousal tucked into her as random people shifted around them, the crowd unaware of Fiona's desire to flow into his fire like glass over flame. She could imagine being in this same position in the dark of night, her legs wrapped around him, urging him inside, moving with every thrust, every slick demand.

She hadn't been attracted to anyone like this in years. Hadn't wanted to rub against them in a packed room, hardly caring what anyone else thought.

For a second, Fiona dipped against him, struggling against the thick moisture of a people-choked room, the overwhelming buzz of being touched so intimately. She was dizzy with the faint scent of leather jacket and…what? Enjoying the fantasy? Fighting to keep her breathing even? Liking the fact that she couldn't manage to gain the upper hand?

But then someone crashed into them, banging Fiona's head against the wall. Knocking some sense into her. *Get a hold of yourself, Fi.*

"Excuse me," she said, trying to make her way past Mac, cold air nibbling at her skin, at the regretful loss of contact.

He gripped her arms tighter. The blood expanded in her veins, thudding, echoing jungle drums, primal and mysterious.

A silly thought occurred to her. What if he didn't let go?

Ridiculous. And tempting, too. But she should have been more worried about other questions.

What if she allowed him to keep her restrained?

It wouldn't happen. Fiona would never fall prey to the whims of anyone—not even this man—again.

She shot a lethal smile at her amused captor. "I'm leaving," she said. "Game over."

"Actually…" Sean McIntyre returned her own slash of a grin. "It's just starting."

2

"WHAT'S JUST STARTING?" she asked, dark eyes cautious, smudged with a hint of something like interest.

"The game."

His grip on her arms tightened even more, and Fiona gasped. Sweet sound, that gasp, making Sean's pulse tumble and growl.

He didn't know she could seem so vulnerable, with her lips parted, her hands grasping at his biceps, clenching, then relaxing.

Releasing.

He didn't want her to go, didn't want to return alone to that party with its confetti-colored balloons and forced gaiety, with Lakota Lang and her spunky ambition.

Instead of letting Fiona escape, he took her by the elbow, away from the crowd to an empty table, where he pulled out a chair for her. With cautious acceptance, she sat, leaning her elbows on the surface, her dress sleeves spreading over the linen like yawning black ink stains.

"What game?" Fiona asked, as he took his own seat.

"The battle of wills between our clients. Or haven't you noticed the storm brewing?"

"Oh, I caught a groan of thunder in the air, all right."

He leaned toward her, close enough so he could feel the wisp of her clothing as it moved against his thigh. "Usually I leave the baby-sitting to the managers, but with these two, I think reconnaissance might not be a bad idea."

And, he added silently, he kind of felt protective toward Lakota Lang. There was still some innocence wrapped in all that tight satin and bravado.

Her date, Brendon Fillmore, was another of Sean's clients. It seemed logical to get both of them some exposure by setting the two strangers up for the night. Brendon's TV show had just been canceled and he needed to stay in the public eye. Lakota needed to cultivate a prime-time image because, with a few night slot TV cameos under her belt, that's where her career was headed. Up.

The kid definitely needed some of Sean's guidance, not that Fiona had to know this.

Her leg moved beneath the table. Back and forth, teasing him with the languid flow of imagination: Her bare thigh skimming up the side of his, her hips grinding against him…

He'd gotten a taste of her body in the hall, when she'd tried to get by him. If he didn't know better, he would have said that Fiona's incidental contact had been just that—a happy accident. But Sean did know better.

She was playing with him.

Voice as low as a murmur of night wind, she said, "I like the way you think. I want to get a feel for how those two react to each other, just to see if we need to worry about a PR explosion. We don't want Linc and Lakota making a scene—unless it's during *Flamingo Beach,* of course."

"Right." Sean glided his forefinger beneath Fiona's chin, directing her gaze across the room. "Watch."

Her breath sighed over the skin of his hand as he lingered, then stroked the side of her neck on his way down.

Damn, he wanted so much more.

Restraining himself—he was on the clock, not a mattress—Sean looked across the room, as well. There, near the very visible dance floor, Lakota and Lincoln worked the crowd, mingling with fans and the press, their backs to each other.

"You have to know they're aware of every move the other one makes," Fiona said.

Just as Sean, himself, was. Every time she swayed her leg so it breezed near his, every time she inhaled and exhaled, for God's sake.

She continued. "What are we watching for?"

"Wicked glances, a foot stuck out just in time to trip another body. They're getting closer and closer to each other. My sixth sense is vibrating."

And that wasn't all.

She turned to him, her voice close enough to buzz around his ear. "I bet Lakota strikes first."

"Lakota? She's got no reason." He turned his head,

bringing his lips closer to Fiona's cheek. "Lincoln's the one who got dumped. I'm sure he's up for a little revenge."

"Linc?" Her warm laugh sizzled his skin. "He's harmless. She's the one who's almost quaking with pent-up hostility. Look at the way she keeps flicking a gaze over her shoulder. She knows he's there, can probably hear his jokes, and I'm betting that his popularity with the fans is killing her."

He tensed, wanting to defend his client, but Fiona's knee had just scratched along his thigh, a slow and deliberate move leaving a wake of burning need in his belly.

Concentration wasn't in the cards tonight.

"Lakota's got enough confidence to keep Lincoln from getting to her," he said.

She slanted her body toward him, bringing her knee back into contact with his body. She nudged it over the top of his shin, then in between his legs.

In reaction, he trailed a hand over her thigh, resting it on that naughty knee. She laughed, a throaty touché from the master.

"Lakota's going to be the first one to cause trouble," she said. "Mark my words."

He glanced at his client. Slinky Versace dress, bedhead red hair, siren makeup. Sure, he wouldn't put it past Lakota Lang to mess with Lincoln Castle, but with Fiona's thigh underneath his hand, with his thumb easing along the inside, seeking a hint of toned muscle, of moist acceptance, he wasn't in a cut-and-dry mood.

He wanted amusement.

"Care to bet on that?" Sean asked, loyal to his client.

"What? That Lakota's going to rile Lincoln first?" Her smile blossomed. "What's the winner get?"

He pressed his hand higher, fingers creeping to her midthigh. Fiona stretched her leg, leaning into him, biting her lip and lowering her gaze in a steamy pause of expectation.

"When I win," he said, "you'll do a task of my bidding."

"Or vice versa."

She removed his touch by sweeping her leg over the other one, crossing them at the knees, keeping him out of further trouble.

A rusty laugh escaped him. "You think Lincoln will keep his cool and ignore Lakota."

She sat a little straighter, and he could tell that she wasn't quite as cocky as she wanted to let on.

"He never fails me," she said.

The blood beat through his hands, filling their emptiness. What he'd give to cup her curves against his palms.

He leaned back in his chair, trying to pretend Fiona didn't affect him. But the awareness between them was too potent to ignore.

It was bad form to be screwing a co-worker. But at this point, he didn't care.

As he chided himself, he found that they didn't have to wait long for the fireworks to start. A paparazzi photographer whom Sean had arranged to stir up some visibility for his clients appeared, urging the soap stars together for a picture. Lakota cozied up to Lincoln as if they were still lovers.

Pop! After the flash faded, she kept her hold on Lincoln's tuxedo jacket. The man's discomfort was clear—the pained expression, the wooden posture.

Sean perched on the edge of his chair, ready to swing into action if anything happened. The managers were at the stars' sides in an instant, but not before Lincoln lost his cool and liberated himself by shrugging out of his jacket, tossing it over a still-clinging Lakota's head.

As he stalked away, several photographers caught her flipping the clothing off her head and bundling into it, then rubbing her hands up and down her arms as if she'd been cold and Lincoln had lovingly loaned her some warmth.

Fiona made a sound of disgust. "You know she started that. Probably said something to goad him."

"Hey," Sean said, grinning. "The only evidence I saw was Lincoln's tux flying through the air to land on my poor client. Quick thinking on her part, huh? She almost does our jobs for us. I'll make sure *Soap Opera Digest* or *US Magazine* has a picture of Lakota in Lincoln's jacket. I can see the caption now—'She's got his love to keep her warm!'"

"Spare me. I'll arrange it so Lincoln is linked with Nicole Kidman, a much classier redhead."

By the tone of her voice, he knew she wasn't thrilled about losing this battle.

"I'll ignore that slight and go easy on you," he

said. "What did the winner of our wager get? Oh, yeah. You have to cater to my whims."

He paused, taking great pleasure at how her dark eyes widened, then narrowed.

A grin quirked his mouth. "Fetch me a drink. Whisky on the rocks."

Fiona stiffened, apparently affronted by the command in his voice.

Sean lifted up his hands, such the good guy. "I could've called in a much more…interesting…prize."

She hesitated, then swept a long look over his body, her gaze like feathers winging from his toes to his neck, leaving a trail of rough tickles.

"I suppose you're right," she said. "But this isn't the end of it. I don't like to lose."

As she left, she winked, her thick eyelashes lending an air of wanton flirtation.

He watched her walk away, unable to tear his eyes off her, off the clingy material of her dress and how it molded those thighs he'd explored, that *ass*.

There was no way he'd get through this night, not without some kind of sexual release. And if getting her into bed made for a tougher workplace tomorrow, then that's how it'd be. He was willing to sacrifice p.c. office protocol for Fiona.

God, she'd be worth it.

This had never happened before, him pursuing someone in the office. Sure, there had been the occasional loaded gesture with an administrative assistant, with a client. But he'd never crossed the line professionally.

Until now.

Work had always mattered too much. He'd spent years being myopic in his pursuit of success. But lately...

Lately it didn't seem to matter as much as the fulfillment of all the fantasies he'd conjured about Fiona Cruz since she'd va-va-voomed into his life yesterday.

Soon, she returned with a flute of champagne for her, a martini for him.

He lifted an eyebrow as she sat. "Not whisky."

A tart smile. "The occasion—and that hot tux—calls for a more sophisticated cocktail. Hollywood's all about image."

"You didn't follow my orders. That means you still owe me."

"Do I?" She watched him over the rim of her glass as she took a sip.

He shrugged, swigged from his drink. Not bad. She knew his tastes, didn't she?

"You always rebel against authority in this way?" he asked.

"I told you, Lakota was the instigator. You didn't win anything."

And she didn't like losing. "Go on. We both know better."

She oh-so-gently set down her flute, so slowly that Sean knew he was in trouble.

"I propose a new bet."

"Clearly losing rankles you more than you'll admit."

"I've got Linc in my sights right now," she said,

ignoring his jibe. "He's fully in control and unruffled. Lakota didn't get to him, you see. But I'm going to bet your client is so hot under the collar she'll try to make Linc jealous. I hear that's her modus operandi."

He couldn't dispute her comment, but he still knew Lakota had ample brains and wouldn't make him lose. "And I'm supposed to wager that Lincoln does something to make Lakota jealous first? Hell, yeah, my money's on him to blow it."

"We'll see. Linc's a *professional.*"

With practiced skill, Sean reached out, running a thumb over her collarbone as she watched him. He dipped the thumb under her bra strap. Toyed with it. Her pulse fluttered against his skin.

"What does the winner get?" he asked.

She glanced at his hand, then back at him. "When I win, you tell me something secret about yourself."

"Or the other way around. I've been wondering what you wear to bed anyway."

It was out there now. She could either tell him to back off and he'd respect her wishes, or she could take up the gauntlet. Her call.

Fiona's eyes went soft, and Sean could have sworn that he'd passed some test. Did she appreciate that he'd laid the choice in her lap?

Instead, she said, "Lakota's got fifteen minutes to lose the bet for you, Mac."

A smile spread over his mouth, and they locked gazes, the promise of tonight and what could happen in the wee hours after the party stretching between them.

As Fiona coolly glanced away from him, making it a point to watch Lincoln and Lakota across the room, the DJ put the pedal to the metal with the music, cranking up the volume. People gradually wandered onto the floor, shedding jackets, dancing, bumping against each other.

Ten minutes passed, but Lakota and Lincoln remained apart. Good girl. She wouldn't do anything to jeopardize her cultivated image, not after he'd put her through all that media combat training.

Then again, maybe he'd spoken too soon. In the near distance, Lakota was arrowing a sly glare in her ex-boyfriend's direction.

It was as if Lincoln felt the sting of Lakota's eyes, because he glanced over at her, their gazes meeting. Sean knew that look.

Wounded, open.

The kind of expression his dad had worn for years, sitting across from his mom's empty chair at the dinner table while Sean and his two sisters took care of the food, the bills, the anguish.

Across the room, Lakota smirked, then turned back to her crowd of admirers, leaving Lincoln hanging.

Sean refrained from toasting her expertise. Clever woman, toying with Lincoln. A lot like Fiona.

Lincoln grabbed a nearby woman's hand and led her to the dance floor, provoking Lakota first, thus assuring Sean's victory in his wager with Fiona. Obviously affronted, Lakota followed suit, partnered with her own weapon of choice—Brendon Fillmore, who'd been courting his own fans with his soft-rebel persona.

Great.

"Dance off," said Sean.

"Let me guess. Lakota's the Shark, Lincoln's the Jet." Her voice was resigned.

He shrugged.

She sighed, a clear white flag of surrender. "I wear girls' tighty-whitie undies."

"You wear ugly underwear to bed?"

"They're made for women, and they're extremely cute. You know, bun-huggers?"

Lust sucker punched him once again. "Fiona, I'm surprised. I expected you to confess a fondness for black-net bodysuits or satin nightgowns. But…"

The image clouded his mind. Fiona, with her long legs showcased by a pair of those clinging panties. With her torso bare, breasts full and throbbing for his touch.

She mock-glared at him. "You're developing a nasty habit of winning."

"That's the way I like it."

Though she seemed to be joking, Sean wondered if she wasn't telling the truth.

"You know," he said, "there's a hole-in-the-wall bar on the corner. Quiet. Secluded."

"Meaning?"

"You're a smart woman."

Fiona stared at him, as if considering the offer. Self-aware ladies knew a night like this probably wouldn't end with a drink. Not with the way he and Fiona were offering those testing swipes.

But before she could answer, Sean felt the frigid

fingers of his business sense strumming the back of his neck. He contained a shiver, then turned around.

Lakota and Lincoln had come toe-to-toe on the dance floor, and it wasn't a *West Side Story* moment, either. She'd left Brendon dancing by himself in order to confront Lincoln, her hand splayed over her ex's chest, nails bared like claws. For his part, Lincoln was holding strong, trying to play off the contact. But before Sean could get out of his chair, the managers had pulled the two apart.

Lakota's handler, Carmella Shears, shot him a glare. Back to the ever-present office.

"Looks like I need to get busy seeing that Lakota smiles for the cameras on the way out." He rose from his chair. "I'm off to help her handler lock her away for the night."

Fiona followed his example and stood. "Have fun tucking her in."

"I don't get involved with clients." But he would mix business with pleasure if given the chance. With Fiona, that is.

He started to leave, then on the spur of the moment, turned back around. "Bailey's. That's what the place on the corner is called."

And, without waiting for her answer, Sean moved toward his troublemaking soap star, feeling Fiona's eyes track him with every step he took away from her.

HE'D WON EVERY BET, damn him.

Fiona had hailed a cab from Linc's house near Griffith Park, where she'd comforted him and talked him down from his doomed meeting with Lakota. Now, as she traveled to her apartment by The Farmer's Market, she stewed over Mac's victory streak.

Sure, he could've really fried her over the flames if he were less of a gentleman. Could've asked her to do something deliciously ridiculous, like flash her breasts in the crowded room. Or was that *her* fantasy machine at work?

Whatever the case, she'd told him she didn't like to lose, and that had been the truth. Fiona had been raised to compete, growing up in a household of three brothers, where they'd all had to vie for attention. Maybe she'd absorbed a lot of testosterone over the course of the years. Who knew?

But she certainly didn't like sitting in the loser's column.

They were approaching Hollywood Boulevard and Bailey's, the bar Mac had mentioned. Her body sang with longing as they got closer. Closer. Passing it by.

Was he waiting there?

And what would happen if she walked in? Sat down?

They'd end up in someone's bed.

A tremble of remembrance riffled through her body, recalling his hand on her leg, in between her thighs.

She wanted him there. Everywhere.

Handling him at work wouldn't be a problem. She'd enjoyed an office affair or two and had always controlled the situation with discreet grace. No one got hurt; that was her mantra.

So why was this any different? Because she needed this gig? Needed to feel successful again?

She was on her way up, and nothing, not even Sean McIntyre, was going to stop her. She could have her cake and eat it, too, just like any man in her business.

"Please turn around," she said to the driver. "There's a bar. Bailey's."

"I know it." The man whipped around the cab, probably thinking she was indecisive, mind-scrambled.

And she was, wasn't she? Deliriously, ecstatically giddy with flashbacks of Mac's corded chest against hers, the chiseled bulges of his arms holding her captive. Controlling her when *she'd* always been the one calling the shots.

The driver dropped her off in front of a sign with a neon-lined martini and olive, and she paid him. As he left, the motor revving into the distance, Fiona took a deep breath, walked into the dark recesses of the bar.

It was a real funky joint: a slim cigarette case lined with half-empty bottles, the aroma of salt and gin, anonymously low lighting and faux-leather upholstery gleaming in the shadows. The jukebox near the back played a Doors tune—"People Are Strange"—and a few suited patrons splayed their bodies over bar stools.

A dead-end weeknight. Her dead end, too.

Mac was among the barflies, ensconced in a booth, discarded tuxedo jacket slouched over the seat, his expansive back to the door. She knew his choice of location was purposeful—not too eager, not too concerned if she showed up or not.

She laughed to herself, then took the first confident step toward him, feeling the gazes of the male customers. Her power grew with every collected, silent compliment.

When she arrived at his seat, he didn't acknowledge her at first. Part of the game, she knew, the pretense of not having the other person on your mind for the past hour and a half. Instead, he kept his eyes on the wall across from him, gaze trained on a picture of a man who could've been the bar's owner posing with Marcus Allen in a Raider's football uniform. One of Mac's hands enfolded a glass of amber liquid—probably that damned whisky he'd wanted her to fetch earlier.

"Drinking alone?" she asked.

Finally, he glanced up. "Thought I would be."

Was that relief written in the tough-life lines of his face? There was something about his expression—the stumbling slant of his mouth, the laconic curve of an eyebrow… She didn't dare hope he was that happy to see her.

His mien returned to its regular programming: gunslinger calm mixed with roguish promise. Then he motioned to the space opposite. "Did you sing Lincoln a few lullabies?"

She slid into the booth. "He's a big boy. Lakota didn't rattle him as much as his manager did, lecturing him about comebacks and all that fun stuff."

"Right." Mac turned to the bartender and ordered her a sour apple martini. Turned back around to flash her a shit-eating grin.

So he was returning the favor from their first bet, flying against her wishes just to get the best of her. Playful boy. Luckily she liked his choice in beverages.

"You actually showed up," he said.

The words had a lonely ring to them, and Fiona's heart tilted on its axis. Lopsided, off center.

"How could I resist?" she asked. "You practically begged."

He laughed, probably not feeling the need to correct her. Fiona was certain that Sean McIntyre never had to plead with a woman, but she could see how it might be the other way around.

"So…" she said.

Silence, as the bartender slid her drink onto the table. She didn't touch it.

Mac waited for the man to leave, then reclined against the seat's cracked leather, narrowing his sharp green eyes. Assessing her intentions?

"Tell me why you're here, Fiona Cruz."

Her breath caught in her throat. Then, she eased her arms onto the table, leaning toward him, knowing good and well that she was showing cleavage, reveling in the power as his eyes strayed there.

"You asked," she said, "and I came."

He grinned again, and her heart did a belly flop, a scalding, breathtaking plunge.

"And come you did. But hopefully not for the last time tonight."

Highly entertained, she smiled right back at him.

3

FIONA SHOOK HER HEAD. "You think I'm going to hop right into the sack with you."

"You haven't thought about it?"

The crimson light from a vintage beer sign fizzed on, suffusing Mac's steady gaze. A second later, it blinked off, as if too weary to put out the effort.

She pressed her breasts against the table, rubbing a little, watching the undisguised hunger of his posture: his wide shoulders arched forward, arm muscles straining against the white of his rolled-up shirt-sleeves. Poised like a predator. Practiced and ready.

"Mac," she said, "let's stop circling each other and be direct. I like men. I like those ridges right above the hipbones. I like kissing my way down a hard chest until I get to the belly button, where I can feel the ab muscles clench with each touch of my lips. I like the feel of a man's back as his shoulders bunch and flex." She paused. "But there are also things I don't like. Pretty words designed to get me into bed. Speedos at the beach. Commitment."

He didn't say anything for a moment. Instead, he ran a finger around the rim of his glass, still watching her.

She tried not to think about what that finger could be doing to her body within the next hour.

Finally, he spoke. "I don't wear Speedos."

"Not many American men make that mistake."

"And I'm wondering how we're going to manage the boss man when he finds out that I made you purr tonight."

Oh.

"Are you assuming that you're going to have the chance?"

He lifted his drink, toasted her. "I'm banking on it."

Cocky. God, she liked that in a man.

As he swigged his whisky, she suggestively ran a finger along the stem of her own martini glass. "Just so we have an understanding, we wouldn't talk about our…extracurricular activities…inside the office. *If* it were to happen."

He pushed his glass away, though it still had plenty in it. "Discretion is the better part of fooling around."

She couldn't believe they were sitting here, talking about this so calmly, not yet tearing each other's clothes off and rolling over the intimate, scarred table. But the verbal foreplay was nice, making her swollen, wet, in need of release.

She wiggled in her seat a bit. "So I can count on you to keep this quiet?"

"As long as we know what to expect of each other, I think we'll do fine."

Expectations. Back when she'd been in love with Ted, she'd cherished a lot of those. Fidelity, everlasting love. Things you saw in romantic movies. Things fairy tales trained young girls to require in a relationship.

She had no expectations now. None except secrecy and lack of commitment.

"If we're laying down some ground rules here, what do you want from me?" she asked.

He reached across the table, positioning a long finger over the one she was using to fondle the martini glass's stem.

"From you?" A graveled chuckle. "Don't worry, Fiona. I'm not the house-in-the-suburbs, two-point-three children and an SUV-in-the-garage type. I'd want to love you for the moment, but nothing beyond that."

The words dug into her, left her hollow. Though she'd been encouraging him to tell her he didn't want anything serious, some tiny, princess-hopeful cell in her body hungered to be romanced, valued in the long run.

Maybe even loved.

But she was beyond that. Love was in the cards for some people—they were meant for marriage, babies. Fiona Cruz was the exception, the yin to normalcy's yang.

"I appreciate your honesty," she said, forcing some moxie into her tone.

He took both of her hands, and she sat up from her cleavage-show hunch. Here it went, the seduction. The part where he sketched patterns over her skin, warmed her palms with temporary affection.

Good. As always, the predictable contact would take away the sting. Would help her refocus on physical pleasure, pure and simple.

Nevertheless, excitement beat in her chest, lower, where it pooled, boiled, bubbled.

"Is there anything you want from me?" he asked, a glint in his eyes.

She hesitated. "Just your vow that when it's over, it's over. No randy winks as you pass my office, no veiled comments to colleagues."

"Can do."

"Good." A quiver passed through her, twanging, vibrating. "I don't ever want to end up like Lakota and Linc."

"What? Warped from the illusion of love?"

Damaged? she added silently.

His comment had a biting snap to it, like the business end of a whip. Did Mac hide his own disappointments, his own reasons for playing the field without settling?

"Something like warped," she said. "I know Linc was over the moon for Lakota. She was more open in those days, and I think there was genuine affection there. But Linc had a complex. 'What if she loves the star and not me?' he'd always ask."

"Lakota seems viperish, but I think she wasn't always that way. She's a sweet girl underneath it all."

Fiona smiled. "A fresh-scrubbed innocent?"

"Believe it or not."

All this talking was killing her, but Fiona didn't want to seem desperate, yanking him out of the bar as if she hadn't had sex in months. Which she actually hadn't. After miscalculating what her client needed during her last job, she'd concentrated on succeeding in a new one, putting sex…and emotions, she supposed…on the back burner.

Now, she'd wait for *him* to make the first move. After all, there was pride to consider.

Mac reached across the small table, threaded his fingers through hers. The gesture touched her, striking her as somewhat tender, testing. Without thinking, she tightened her grip on him, then loosened it, ashamed of being so needy, so easily charmed.

"Lakota," she said, swallowing away the surge of feeling, "called off the relationship because she thought Linc was cheating. He wasn't, of course. You'll never find a more constant guy than he is. But she got territorial and overreacted by leaving him altogether."

"Par for the course," said Mac, focusing attention on just one of her hands now, stroking the rough tips of his fingers up the inside of her arm, back down.

White heat spiraled through her bloodstream, infecting her with passionate discomfort.

"What do you mean?" she asked, slightly breathless. "Are you saying women can't get through a liaison without some measure of possessiveness?"

"That's right."

"You're wrong."

He cocked a golden brow. "Am I?"

"Absolutely." Fiona pushed away his fingers. "There're women who can be just as cavalier as men.

Not in a relationship necessarily, because, by definition, those are supposed to be based on feelings. But when it comes to sex, females don't necessarily have to get attached.''

''I've never seen evidence of that.'' He glanced at her arm, then brazenly slid his finger down one of her veins until he came back to her palm. ''Every woman I've been with has shown some sign of wanting to go beyond sex, even if it's a hesitation as you kiss goodnight.''

''Did you ever take them up on their willingness, subtle as it might be?''

''No.'' The word grated out. Then he grinned. ''That's where the liaison ends, when someone gets ideas. Cut it out before she gets her heart broken, I say.''

''I agree.'' She really did. Absolutely.

''Sounds like you think the rule doesn't apply to you. That you can escape unscathed after sex.''

''I can.''

''Bullshit.''

Fiona shook her head. ''Poor guy. You operate under some fearful misconceptions.''

''You're telling me that, after having sex with a man for, say a month, you could leave the affair without…''

''…becoming possessive or territorial? Yes, I can. I *have*.''

He laughed again, combing his other hand through his dark blond hair, the strands sticking up, ruffled and boyishly attractive, contrasting with the darkness in the center of his irises. "If you hadn't lost every bet we initiated tonight, I'd wager that, given one month with me, you'd become emotionally attached."

Her heart chopped against her ribs, and her hand inadvertently fisted around his busy finger. "Well, that's damn arrogant."

He cast a pointed glance at the intensified contact, and she let go.

But even after a second, she missed the feel of him. His callused skin. The way he was big enough to hide her fingers in his grasp, cradling her. Just holding her.

"Wouldn't you love to see me lose?" he asked.

Yes, she would, so much she could almost do a victory dance right now. And she *could* win. No problem. She'd spent the past few years being emotionally distant, if not physically warm and willing, after sex.

"If we embarked on such a philosophical experiment," she said, "what would the winner get? Wait. I'd love to go to the Caribbean. It's time for a vacation."

"Sounds good. A Caribbean getaway of the winner's choice, all expenses paid by the loser."

"This is getting interesting, because I could kick your ass in this bet."

He seemed grandly amused, his full mouth tilted at an angle, half-hidden by the scruffy drifter's stubble surrounding his lips. "You'd be in love with me before you knew it."

Though his comment came off jokingly, Fiona wasn't so sure he didn't mean what he said. Then again, hadn't he mentioned he ended his affairs before they went too far?

Not that it mattered. Fiona didn't do love. Wouldn't happen. She had this wired.

"So," he said, "how will I know I've won the bet?"

She laughed low in her throat, a hint of the purr he'd promised her earlier. "You'll see it in my eyes, Mac. The fact that you've lost, I mean."

"Then we do this scientific eye check after every time I've been inside you?"

She could almost feel him now, filling her, slipping in and out while the sheets got torn off the bed corners. "That's logical enough."

Silence, punctuated by another jukebox Doors song. "The End."

Which should have told her something.

A wave of yearning stretched Fiona out of the booth, bringing her to her feet. She started to walk away from him, slowly, zinging that extra sway into her stride.

She glanced over her shoulder, discovering his gaze on her derriere. The naked desire in his look turned her blood to steam.

"The bet starts now," she said, crooking her finger at him in summons. "Game on."

She turned around, moving away, knowing he was going to follow.

THEY'D TAKEN A TAXI to his rented place off Melrose Avenue because she'd requested they go where he lived.

He understood her reasoning, because he liked to go to his lover's place, as well. It gave a person control.

Done with the sex? Hey, I've got an early meeting tomorrow, time for me to leave.

The visitor dictated the schedule.

But, with Fiona, Sean didn't mind. He wanted her in his bed as soon as possible, no matter the location.

Hell, he'd have taken her on the way to his home if he hadn't wanted to make a point.

To show her he had patience and would win the bet.

Yeah, the wager was a good way to get Fiona to do what he wanted. And, no, he had no intention of making her fall for him. As usual, the second he saw emotion, he'd stop the affair.

A sultry midnight mist had fallen over the streets, lamps casting a bourbon tinge over the sidewalks. Jazz music—heavy on the drumbeats—beckoned from the open windows of a neighbor's house. When they walked through the gate to his Spanish Renaissance Revival home with the palms and Birds of Paradise plants lining the sidewalk, Sean tried not to rush through the door. Instead, he took his time, allowing her to walk in front of him, her hips ticking back and forth like a pendulum, counting down the moments.

She sauntered up the steps, leaning against the stucco wall near the door, waiting for him to unlock the iron grating.

They hadn't said a damned word all the way here, and the silence ate at him.

He pulled open the iron, then pushed in the heavy wood door. His pulse thudded in his ears as she glided past, the swish of her black, airy dress coaxing him to follow her inside.

As he reached for the lights, Fiona grasped his wrist, pulling him away from the entrance, bolting him against the wall. The door slapped shut, darkening the room further. But the sheer-gold moonlight allowed him a peek of her while she pressed against him, body to body.

White curtains billowed away from his open window, the linen flirting, dancing over her dusky skin. Her eyes wide, black as a dreamless sleep, she asked, "Ready for me, Mac?"

Tousled voodoo hair. Jazz drums. The smoldering aroma of her mango-scented skin reminding him of lush breezes and oceans lapping at the sand.

In response he planted a hand in her loose curls, tightened gently, guided her mouth to his in a searing kiss.

She moaned against his lips, opening, rubbing, nipping at him. And, as he devoured her in return, he slipped a hand to the small of her back, tracing the curve of spine, trailing downward. His fingers sketched over her fruit-plump ass, palming it under the cheek and thrusting her against his growing erection.

Damn, he was hard—too ready and willing. If he wasn't careful, he was going to spill himself all over the carpet like a twelve-year-old on his first date with a *Playboy* centerfold.

Sean slowed the pace. Tilting Fiona's head with his other hand, he eased his tongue into her mouth, running it over the edge of her teeth, circling, tasting a memory of champagne sweetness.

She came up for air, leaning her head against his jaw. "Your stubble burns," she said. "But in a good way."

"I'm not about to stop and shave it off."

"Even if I asked you to?"

"You really—"

She pounced, cut him off with her lips.

They sipped at each other, chafing against the wall, knocking into end tables and anemic wooden chairs.

The force of their kiss heating up again, he whipped her around, gently yet firmly placing her against the wall now. Raising her arms above her head, he stared down at her.

"You're a damn good kisser, Fiona," he said around the holes of his breathing.

She panted, too. "And vice versa. I like a good, old-fashioned lip lock. Did I leave that off my list?"

The list. Images of her skimming her lips down the length of him shuddered an emergency alarm through every cell of his body.

Unable to hold back, he rocked against her, urging his cock into the crevice between her legs.

Her arms lost their bone structure, melted down until they rested on top of her head.

Seizing the opportunity, he roamed south, thumbs dragging over the pounding column of her neck, over her swollen breasts, the softness of her stomach, to her thighs. There, he slid upward, under her dress.

Garters. He should've known she'd be wearing thigh-high stockings and a belt. A woman with fire like Fiona's wouldn't settle for less, not even on a weeknight.

Sean leveled out his breathing. *Take it easy, man.*

With hard-won deliberation, he unsnapped one garter. Then the other. Lifted her skirt so he could glimpse the retro-sexy lingerie.

Oh, yeah. Dark lace and long legs.

"Men are so visual," she said on a sigh.

"And you use that to your advantage."

He pushed the dress to her waist, slipped a thumb between her legs to slide against her damp panties. He pressed against her clit, massaging, daring her to explode before he did.

She sank against the wall, biting her lip as she smiled and squeezed her eyes shut. As he exerted more pressure, Fiona started to move her hips, swaying in time to the stimulation.

How was he going to last? Already moisture was building on the tip of his penis. He could feel it.

With something close to a groan, he stroked his fingers into her underwear, eased them inside of her. In, out, faster, thumb working her, moaning, sliding...

She embraced him again, bit his ear, making him dizzy, disoriented. His lobe was his Achilles' heel.

Without warning, she'd forced him backward, and he held on to her, backing into a chair. She pushed off with a triumphant gasp, and before he knew it, he was seated, pulse pounding in his crotch.

He laughed, intrigued by this tug-of-war. "The wall wasn't comfortable enough for you?"

Her smile echoed his mirth. Instead of answering, she plucked off her ankle-strap heels, propped her foot on the chair's arm and slicked off one stocking, dangling it in front of him. Moonlight filtered through it, clouding his vision. She allowed the silk to shiver to the ground.

He stretched in the chair, accommodating her strip-teasing, wishing she'd get on his lap so he could thrust himself inside her.

When the other stocking was done for, she wiggled out of the garter belt, kicking it behind her. His hands itched for her to join him on the chair, but she pulled another fast one by turning around, shimmying, glancing over her shoulder.

"Get over here," he said, the words graveled with raw need.

She sent him a saucy glance, resting her chin on her shoulder as she appeared to unbutton the front of her dress. A faint jazz-drum tattoo accompanied her, lending a laconic sensuality to her undulating hips.

Encouraged, Sean unbuttoned the top of his pants. With a teasing laugh, she reversed onto his lap, smoothing her rump back over his thighs until he had his chest near her spine. Her legs were spread apart, straddling him.

"Ever had a lap dance?" she asked.

The breath whooshed out of him. "You think I'm a monk or something?"

"Do you like lap dances?"

He muttered a frustrated curse, hating and loving her playful pokes at seduction. With one smooth scoop, he had her flush against him, one leg over the chair's arm, his fingers tracing the inside of her thighs.

"Wanna tease me some more?" he asked, urging her back against his arousal. It beat against her rear, pounding out its demands.

She wiggled in answer, exciting him to the point of bursting. But he controlled himself, wanting to win this power struggle, wanting to end the contest while enfolded in her spasming, slippery heat.

As she gyrated, grinding up, then down his lap, reaching back to caress his hair, his face, he held on to her hips, working them to and fro. She arched away from him, causing him to reach up, cup her lacy-bra-bound breasts, feel her nipples harden between his fingers, under his thumbs.

One last brush of her ass against his crotch, and he'd had enough.

He picked her up, laying her face up on the floor. "I'm taking over now."

"So you think."

With skillful finesse, he delved inside her dress, undoing her bra, freeing her breasts. He took one in his mouth, sucking, tonguing it.

"Dammit," she said, threading her fingers through his hair. Pressing herself to him, she wrapped her legs around his body.

He'd imagined the cage of her legs, the strain of their bodies absorbing each other's sweat. And fantasy wasn't nearly as good as this.

They kissed again, pausing only to tear Fiona out of her dress, panties and bra, to pull him out of his shirt and pants. Bare naked, both of them.

She breathed into his ear. ''Got a—?''

''—Yeah.''

He attacked his pants pocket, fought with his wallet, took out the condom.

She tugged it away from him, running a finger under his cock, making him grab for the carpet with the lightning-flash electricity of her touch. Then she paused to rub her thumb over the tip of him, spreading the beads of semen that had accumulated.

''You're gonna feel so good, Mac.''

Her fingers traced his balls, and he tilted back his head, fighting for restraint.

She pushed him backward, until he lay prone on the carpet, then slid the rubber over him with a single, smooth caress.

Legs encasing him, she rested her hands on his shoulders, using her nails to abrade him. Then she sat on his belly, her nether lips opening over his skin, sticking to him with her juices. She moved her mouth up to his head, slicking down his body with the laziness of a summer cloud traveling the sky. Her dark hair rained over his face, his chest, his lower stomach.

He shuddered deep within his belly, and the violence of his reaction spurred him into motion. He grasped her hips, urgently leading her onto his shaft, impaling her.

She sucked in a breath, bending back her head, body waving to and fro. Then she flipped her hair, leaned forward, furling and unfurling over him, working him to a frenzy with increasing thrusts.

While she pulsated against him, he watched her breasts move with every thrash, her hair swing and mingle with the sweat on her shoulders, her arms and chest.

He tore into her, their bodies drumming and stretching to the saxophone rhythm of a July night, skin misted, slick, sensitive. Inside, she was hot and fluid, a vortex of fluttering muscles that swallowed him in a roar.

But he held back, straining for control, as she moved on top of him, churning, grasping for satisfaction.

He plunged deeper, watching her face, the silent *o* of her mouth, the lazy roll of her neck. Fascinated, he added the play of his fingers to her mounting orgasm, working her, delving between her wet lips. Pressing, on, off, around, up, feeling the base of his cock as it slipped in and out of her. Getting even more turned on by the thought of disappearing, being enfolded by her heat, being sucked in and out.

In.

Out.

She shuddered, arched backward until her long hair winged over his legs, then she groaned, a long, sated signal of fiery contentment. After a jagged breath, she prowled back over him until she lay flush against his length, eye to eye, predator to predator.

It was all he could stand.

A growl wrenched from his lungs as he turned her over, her back on the carpet. She laughed and circled him with her endless legs. Beyond restraint, he hammered into her, hearing her breathe a soft, instinctive "oh" every time he drove home. Deeper.

They were a tangle of arms and legs. She bit into his neck, climaxing again and spearing an aching spasm through his dick.

"Oh, yeah," she said, grinding hard against him, encouraging his own implosion. "Come on."

He burst, spilling himself into the rubber in a swirl of mindless light, filling the condom. Filling her.

He was spent, but he didn't want to leave. She was holding him there, wrapped around every aftermath throb. It was the only kind of embrace he could bring himself to accept, and Fiona seemed to understand that as she held him inside her, their muscles clenching, unclenching, weakening. Letting go.

They lay side by side, panting, skin-slicked and intimate, watching each other. He'd found a perfect partner, hadn't he?

Sean smoothed back her hair, peered into her eyes with taunting exaggeration.

He froze. Did he see a flicker, a flame?

Whatever it was, the warmth was doused in an instant.

Sighing, she shut her lids, turned away her face.

"The bet." She blinked open again, all of a sudden coy, playful. "What do you find, Sherlock?"

Now? Nothing but a wink and a smile. Nothing more than he'd asked for at the bar. "A whirlpool of emotion," he said, trying to play it off as if it didn't matter.

And it didn't. That tiny seed of disappointment in his belly, growing among the awakening aftershock shivers, didn't mean anything. He wanted it this way. No attachment, no bonding.

But wasn't she feeling anything? Hadn't he seen *something?*

She rose to an elbow, her breasts moving, tempting him to regroup and go another round with her. But she was having none of it, apparently, because she got to her knees, reached for her clothes.

"That was amazing," she said, chipper as a Girl Scout who'd just gotten a badge for creating rug burn.

Maybe too chipper?

Shifting position, he felt the carpet beneath him stroke his tender backside. He'd pay for this later.

He murmured an agreement to her "amazing" comment, leaning his head back into the cradle of his arms.

She was actually leaving.

Her efficiency was astounding. She called for a cab, then started to get into her clothes.

"Since you haven't won any Caribbean vacations yet," she said, "when do we try this again?"

In a half hour? "Whenever you want."

"Okay." She finished dressing. "I'll catch you

bright and early tomorrow at work. We'll see what happens afterward.''

She swept one last look over his sweat-decorated body then made for the door. There, she hesitated, and he propped himself on an elbow, waiting.

When she opened her mouth, no words came out. Instead, her gaze fell to the floor, and she laughed a little.

''You can't hear it, but I really am purring inside,'' she said softly.

''Isn't that what I promised?'' He ignored the spark in his chest. ''Wait for the cab in here.''

For a second, she didn't move. Then, ''No. It's one of those beautiful, warm California nights. I'll be fine.''

She opened the door, stepped outside. Through the thin dress, he could see her legs, her curvy figure. Then she left. Done. Gone.

His conscience tried to placate him:

Let them go before they start to care. Keep it light. No strings attached.

Sean McIntyre closed his eyes, shutting out the longing for something more.

4

THE TWINGE in Fiona's conscience—as well as the faint vibrations tickling her skin—lasted into the next evening.

And, dammit all if she couldn't keep her mind off Mac. The stiff, damp throb between her legs, the constant replay of their night together, invaded her with intangible heat. Reminding her. Thrilling her.

Taunting her.

In spite of the air-conditioning, Fiona fanned herself, surveying the scene at the Goddess Gallery on Beverly Boulevard. She'd put together a photography show for one of the clients who had been assigned to her by the firm. Terry Oatman, the artist in question, was a washed-up actor who'd done several straight-to-video bombs during the past few years. Two decades ago, he'd been the hippest Ray●Ban-wearing man on the scene, but now, after a bout with drugs and a free-fall from fame, he was sober. Ready to reinvent his image.

And it was her job to make sure he made it again.

Things looked good so far. A few A-list rockers and movie stars had made it to opening night; they wandered through the incense-scented gallery, mingling, drinking the gratis champagne, perusing the black-and-white portraits only when they thought it would matter. Fiona had persuaded a movie magazine to do a layout of Oatman's work and, every few minutes, another flash would light up the white-walled room.

The only person who seemed genuinely interested in something other than being noticed or eating their fill of hors d'oevres was Lincoln, the lone soap star, isolated by his low position on the Hollywood food chain. He wandered the exhibit, considering each photo.

Her throat tightened. He hadn't wanted to talk about last night and what had happened with Lakota, so she'd decided to give him space until he was ready. Give him space because he knew something was up with her, also.

Brother. Could she stop thinking about Mac? She'd managed to extinguish all the sparks he'd ignited in her. Sort of. It was necessary though, because those dangerous bursts of hope and connection rubbed against the emptiness of her better judgment, shocking her system.

Had Mac seen what she'd felt, even for that terrifying second? It'd been a mix of instinctive optimism, the utter happiness of contentment. Of finding an equal.

Fiona leaned against the wall, the black-garbed gallery crowd blurring into one big empty hole.

At least she'd gotten out of his house before she'd surrendered to the moment altogether. The cab had arrived within ten minutes and, with every moment that ticked by, she hoped Mac wasn't looking out the window, seeing her standing by herself. Seeing how much she'd wanted to go back inside to be with him again.

Thank God he'd been called out of the office today, overseeing a star-studded fashion show sponsored by Stellar, making sure all their top talent got tickets, got noticed.

And she'd definitely felt his absence. But only because sex was still on her brain—the comfort of a near stranger, the warmth of another body reassuring her that she was wanted, if only for a short time.

She had everything under control now. Mac was nothing more to her than a bet. An intense flirtation. A day-after, first burn of sensual awareness that cried out for more.

And if he hadn't called her yet, so what? It didn't matter.

Nothing to get territorial about.

Fiona focused again, the room returning to normal, the black hole vanishing, morphing back into her glamour-and-grunge clients. Her real life.

A petite woman clutching a clipboard parted the crowd, rolling her eyes in exasperation as she reached Fiona. Rosie, her assistant.

"Trouble?" asked Fiona.

Rosie's pale cheeks were splotched pink, and strands of her strawberry-blond hair spiked out from the tight bun she wore. Even her off-the-rack suit was a little rumpled. Fiona would have to take the enthusiastic girl shopping if she wanted to get ahead.

"Fiona, Jerry Rute's had too much to drink again, and he's starting to hit on the movie magazine photographer." Rosie adjusted her wire-rimmed glasses. "His handler just took him out the back door."

Jerry Rute. One of those boy band singers who'd turned movie star and didn't quite know how to handle his middling fame.

Fiona kept frustration at bay. "His manager should've taken all those drinks out of his greedy little hands. Isn't that why these stars have entourages? To keep them out of trouble?"

"Or to get them into it."

She stepped out of her corner. "You're learning quickly. Are you sure you want a job that usually requires cleaning up messes instead of preventing them?"

The assistant brightened. Like everyone else in this town, she wore her ambition in her gaze. "I'm sure. Oh, and I'll let the caterers know that we need more fontina risotto balls with that marinara sauce. They're going like hotcakes."

"Thanks, Rosie."

"No problem." The young girl started to dash away, then turned around again, holding up a finger. "By the way, those premiere tickets came through."

A bolt of adrenaline shot through Fiona. Score one for her. This was where she'd regain her shine. If she pleased the ragtag bunch of clients Stellar had dumped on her, more powerful talent would gravitate her way.

She could win their game.

"Excellent work," she said to her assistant, making her glow.

As the young woman darted behind a white wall covered by a mammoth image of an abandoned filling station on Route 66, Fiona couldn't stop an emerging grin.

Let's see, she thought. A limited amount of tickets to the hottest movie premiere in town next week. Who would benefit the most? The actress who was living down a very public struggle with anorexia? The actor whose last film bombed during opening weekend? Or all the B-listers who wanted so desperately to be A-list?

She hated choosing. Hated hearing the client's voice on the phone when they realized they weren't important enough to score the most sought-after prizes of fame.

If only she could please them all.

Lincoln passed into her view as he moved to a new picture.

His posture tore at her: the slightly slouched shoulders of someone who knows he's not wanted at the popular kids' party, the too-intense scrutiny of the art.

Fiona slid up next to him. "See anything you like?"

Linc didn't say anything for a second, then he shrugged, his classy-cool bomber jacket creaking.

"Oatman's got a good eye. Not that any of these people would care."

"It might help if you mingled with 'these people.' Schmoozing is worth its weight in gold. Come on, let's work the room."

He shot her a wry glance. "I'm in soaps. And, guess what? I kind of like being there. You're the one with all the high hopes for me."

Was he angry with her? "You deserve the best, Linc. That's what I want for you."

She felt him take her hand, squeeze it, then let go. "I know."

"Something else is bugging you though."

"Not here, Fi."

"Okay. I got it. You're fine. You big he-man who no want to deal with woman problem."

Another partygoer who happened to be interested in the actual display wandered by them, lingered, then moved on.

Linc stirred, moved closer to Fiona. "I need to stop throwing my whole heart into relationships. It kills me."

Not that he fell in love with every woman he met, but when Lincoln was smitten, he was gone. Completely devoted to the point of *becoming* the other person. His love wasn't of the healthy variety, yet she'd done her best to support him throughout the years.

"You're just that way," she said, keeping her voice low enough to avoid announcing their conversation, loud enough to overcome the soft, live acoustic guitar music being played in the corner by yet another client.

She continued. "You're intense, and someday you'll find a woman who'll accept all your love. But she's not going to be easy to find."

"I smother them, don't I?"

They'd had this heart-to-heart before. "If you're talking about Lakota…"

"Lakota's a free bird, not a clinging vine." He laughed without humor. "The whole 'other woman' deal provided an excuse for her to leave. That's that."

The other woman. The phrase reminded her of Ted, her ex. But in Linc's case, there had been no other. Only Lakota.

Was there more than one woman in Mac's life?

The thought caused Fiona to cross her arms over her chest, but once she realized what she'd done, she returned to her relaxed, isn't-this-a-great-party? position.

Fiona lightly bumped into Linc. "Don't let your-intensity do you in now. Okay? I've told you before to keep your distance from Miss Thang."

"Not likely." He turned away from the picture: two fluffy, coy Maltese dogs sitting in a rusted-out car. "The next script has our first scene together and, surprise! The writers are pairing us up again."

"Ooo. Well, it was inevitable, wasn't it? The fans will go nuts for you two, and the network knows it."

"Fame costs too much. Maybe I should retire." He jerked his chin toward an Oatman portrait of a desert landscape. "I'd like to be this guy, taking pictures for a living. That'd make me happy."

Fiona remembered how he used to take off some weekends just to capture photos. He'd skid back Monday morning in time for class, then develop his own pictures, never showing anyone else but her.

"You can do anything you want to, Linc."

He laughed, dismissed the idea by turning away from the exhibit. "Now that we've hashed out my angst, how about that spark in your eye?"

Fiona took a step back, laughed. "What're you talking about?"

"All right. Have it your way."

"No, I mean…" God, she wanted to talk to him about Mac. Talk to anyone about him. Being naturally more comfortable with guys, she wasn't close to any women, and she definitely wouldn't tell her family. The only confidant she really responded to was Lincoln. "We…"

Another art gazer happened by.

When she was gone, Fiona added, "…You know."

"It's been so long that I don't think I know. Is it love?" he joked.

"Of course not."

"That's right. Love will never again find Fiona Cruz. You'll make sure of it."

The truth pinched at her. "Thanks for being direct."

"Someone needs to be with you. You were wearing more than your sex drive on your sleeve last night."

"That's how I look at all my victims, so don't misinterpret lust as something more."

"Whatever you say."

The movie mag photographer walked by them, obviously searching for a worthy subject. Linc straightened, flashed his brightest, sexiest smile.

The woman reacted to his gesture—what female could resist?—but passed by without a request for a photo.

The snub knocked the breath out of Fiona.

Though Lincoln kept his eyes on the crowd, scanning it as if he'd turned around for that very purpose, she could see the pain floating below the surface. He slowly put his hands in his jacket pockets. He maintained that lethal smile, even though Fiona knew it wasn't real.

"We'll get you there," she said softly.

The smile dimmed, revealing a streak of vulnerability. "If anyone can dig me out of my hole, you can."

Fiona clasped his hands in hers, hardly caring who saw, hardly caring what they would speculate.

And caring way too much that they probably wouldn't bother.

"Six months of staying out of trouble, Lincoln. You've already helped yourself back to the top."

They stayed connected for a moment, until Fiona, thinking she shouldn't stay that way for too long, finally let go.

THREE DAYS and he hadn't called her. Did that make him a creep?

As Sean hopped out of his Jeep and made his way across Pasadena's gas lamp-lined Colorado Bridge, he stifled the urge to toss his damned cell phone off the side of it.

Lakota's manager had kept calling him while he was arranging an *Entertainment Tonight* interview for another client; she'd insisted that he get himself over to a photo shoot he'd secured for Lakota. A shoot for

People magazine's "50 Most Beautiful" issue. What a coup. Unfortunately, they'd requested that she pose with Lincoln Castle, thus upping the interest level for the audience. Ex-lovers reunited on their soap.

He and Fiona had managed to work out the details via their assistants, but this current situation required his personal attention. Probably Fiona's, too.

Dammit, should he have sent flowers? Tapped on her office door to say, "Hey, had a great tumble with you. Wanna go again?"

Did wager etiquette require that sort of thing? Or should he take it at face value—an affair of convenience. Nothing more.

Hell, their bet hadn't said anything about him becoming territorial. And...

You know, he wasn't even going to think along those lines. It'd been a good time. Period.

So why was he so reluctant to see her? To ask when they would resume the contest?

They'd both been too busy to come face-to-face in the office. Or maybe he'd made sure that he was buried under more field work than he could stand.

Damn, he *was* a jerk. A jerk who couldn't stop thinking about her.

Sean approached the screens and lights, the crowd composed of makeup artists, the photographer, the actors and their employees and...

Damn. Fiona *was* here.

She was the only sight he could focus on.

Drawing nearer, he grinned. Summer sunlight gleamed off her dark hair, the subtle wind blowing a strand across her eyes, masking her. She wore a curve-hugging black suit, propping her hands on her hips, but not in a defensive way. As usual, she was cocked at a provocative angle, loose-limbed. Inviting as hell.

As he came to stand in front of her, he thought she sucked in a breath. But then her confident business smile took over, erasing any hint of what had happened between them.

"I knew Lakota would call you, just to one-up Linc."

Cool as the smooth edges of an ice cube, wasn't she?

He sidled closer, forcing her to tilt up her chin so she could meet his gaze. It reminded him of how she'd stood on her toes, flush against his wall, as he'd pressed her upward, onto him.

When he didn't answer, she whipped the hair out of her eyes.

Pow. Her glare sent a punch of need right through him, a reminder of how she'd met him thrust for thrust, driving him further into madness every time she'd urged him, countered him.

"Well, Fiona," he said, dragging out her name just enough to establish the upper hand, "when my client tells me that her demanding co-star won't be photographed from his left side, it tends to throw a kink in the smooth shoot I had planned."

"Did your dainty angel mention that she's been just as ornery?" Fiona faced him straight on. "Linc wanted me here to sort things out, to make sure the crew knows that he's willing to cooperate. Lakota's not his boss. Today, he's taking orders from the magazine. If she continues to bark out commands—''

"—He'll call in the cavalry.''

A muscle in Fiona's jaw twitched. "Listen, Mac. Linc's got more fan mail than anyone else on the soap now, including Lakota. I'm not saying she's jealous—''

"—No?—''

"—but we need to work together on this nightmare. Can we deal with it?''

It. Was she talking about Lakota's and Linc's stubbornness?

Or was she referring to the heat that hung over them?

Sean glanced at Lakota, who was surrounded by her minions, clearly at home with her diva role. Three lampposts down the bridge, Lincoln leaned over the rail, ignoring his own exhausted manager.

These two were going to take up too much of his precious time, weren't they?

Sean didn't turn back to her. "He called and you came running. Either you don't know how to manage your time, or you're the ultimate friend.''

She paused. "That's right. He called, I came. What can I say?''

They weren't talking about Lincoln anymore.

Suddenly, Sean's shirt collar felt too tight, the air caught in his windpipe, choking him.

"Sean!''

Lakota had discovered his presence, and he had to admit that her timing was exceptional.

She wiggled on over to him in high heels, a tight red dress that complemented her Jessica Rabbit hair. Makeup was caked on her face, adding years of sophistication.

"Will you set things straight?" she asked, keeping Fiona in her sights.

Fiona merely sighed and nodded in Lincoln's direction, beckoning to him. "We're going to take care of this ridiculous pissing contest right now."

Lakota's mouth opened, then shut. When she glanced at Sean, he didn't react.

"You and Lincoln can make the image spinning easier for all of us," he said. "Prime-time producers won't want to hire a troublemaker as a regular for their shows. Remember that."

This kept Lakota in check. She desperately wanted to get out of the soaps someday. The sooner the better.

Lincoln came to stand between Fiona and Sean. "Sorry about this, guys."

Sean almost felt sorry for him. He knew how it was when a woman got her dander up. There was no pleasing them. And if you catered to them too much, they took advantage, sometimes even left. Ask his father about that.

"Now," said Fiona. "We're going to get something straight. You two need to think about how you're coming off to the magazine people and all the other professionals you're ticking off."

Lakota watched the ground. "But he—"

"—Oh, no." Fiona wagged a finger. "Don't go all junior high on me."

"Fi," said Lincoln, "this won't happen again. Will it, Kota?"

Kota? Nicknames?

The starlet's head shot up and, for a second, Sean thought he saw her lips flutter into a half smile. Then the tenderness disappeared, replaced by a tight line.

"If you can manage to let me show my best side to the camera without insisting that you show yours, it won't happen again."

Fiona shook her head and spoke to Sean as if the others weren't even there. In a mock-ecstatic voice, she said, "They're both blessed with a perfect right profile. Isn't that convenient?"

The two stars shot a miffed glance at Fiona.

Why was it she'd left her last PR firm? Had she rubbed a client the wrong way? One thing Sean increasingly hated about this job was the amount of butt kissing that went on. What happened to the days when he used to thrive on the fast pace, the accomplishment of seeing his work rise to great heights?

His stars weren't the only things that had lost their luster.

But not Lakota Lang. Not his last chance. "Luckily," he said, "those profiles will get them bigger contracts, better projects."

Fiona pulled an impressed face, still in full sarcastic mode. "I might add that it'll take more than profiles to climb their way up the Hollywood ladder. Talent, bankability, strong work ethic, thinking about how their co-workers might feel... All of those qualities make for a well-rounded entertainer."

Had the co-worker reference been aimed at him? Dammit, she had no idea how many times he'd reached for the phone, wanting to hear her husky voice again, wanting to ask her for another night. Any night.

Without thinking, he said, "Maybe co-workers need to worry about their own business and not bring feelings into it."

Her chin lifted, then lowered. Lakota and Lincoln were strangely silent.

"Well," said Fiona, those plump lips turned up in her permanent smile. "I guess if co-workers had agreed to keep feelings out of the 'office,' so to speak, then it's not a problem."

Lincoln pointed toward the waiting cameras. "I think—"

But Sean couldn't hold back a retort. "Great. If the co-workers understand each other, there's no harm done."

"None at all."

Lakota locked gazes with Lincoln, and they both left without saying goodbye.

Not that Sean or Fiona noticed.

She'd crossed her arms over her chest, inadvertently pushing up her breasts. Or did she know exactly what she was doing?

Blood pumped to his crotch, beating out images of their night together, touch by touch: her smooth skin, whispering under his fingertips. Her nipple, beading against his tongue. The wet folds of her sex, slipping against him.

He watched their clients go back to work, both of

them shifting into acting gear, smiling at each other every time the camera flashed.

Liars. But good ones.

He didn't move, just fixed his gaze on the pseudo-lovers. "I guess I should've called."

Fiona sighed, and even that sounded like an invitation. "That wasn't the deal. I'm just surprised—"

She cut herself off.

"I didn't ask for more?" he finished for her. He faced her, tucking his hands in his pants pockets.

Maybe he'd caught her unaware, but she had a strange look on her face.

Territorial? Possessive?

She made a show of squeezing shut her eyes, smiling. "It doesn't matter. We're mature adults. We can go on with our jobs and forget about what happened after the charity auction."

"Fiona." His voice had a scratch to it, a scraped need.

Her dark eyes widened.

"Dinner," he said, stepping closer to her. "Tonight."

A sidelong glance. A return to the old Fiona, the charmer. The metamorphosis left him dazed.

"Was having me at your beck and call a part of the bet?" she asked.

She ran a hand along her skirt-covered thigh, rendering him capable of nothing but the simplest of sentences.

"I'll pick you up at eight."

"No." Fiona turned, started to walk away. "I'll pick *you* up."

Who was he to argue? "Any way you want it."

Another grin, this one kittenish. Hungry for some cream. "I'll remember that."

With a lingering glance over her shoulder, Fiona tracked him as she left. "One more thing," she said.

He shook his head, caught up in the sway of her voluptuous hips, the length of her legs in that clinging black suit.

She winked. "How about you finish smoothing things over with our stars? I've got other matters to take care of."

Like what? Soaking herself in mango-scented water, preparing to drive him nuts? Picking out another pair of filmy stockings to slide up those curvy legs?

Before he could ask, she was gone, getting into her Miata and zooming out of Pasadena. Back to the office.

Back to their bet.

Sean swallowed, coating a mouth that had gone dry.

5

Tonight, tonight, won't be just any...

Oh, can the hysterical musical monologue, Fiona thought for about the fiftieth time since she'd gone home to shower and primp for dinner.

Dinner. A slight understatement. Mac had made arrangements for a picnic to be served on a rented boat. Talk about going all out.

They'd anchored off the night-blanketed coast of Santa Monica, where the city lights sparkled from the hills, winking like a sky full of wishes. Or of ill-conceived love songs.

Tonight, tonight...

Stop it.

She diverted her attention to the black water that surrounded them. The boat cut through the swells, distancing them from the Santa Monica pier, with its colorful Ferris wheel and roller coaster, which soon looked like the smears of a child's finger painting.

Fiona held her glass of Chardonnay by the stem, judging its pale hue from the light of a tiny lantern Mac had positioned on the cabin's top. She breathed in the tang of ocean mist, enjoying the scene. Mac had spread a linen cloth over the opposite bench, topping it with an assortment of strawberries, watermelon and honeydew melon, shrimp cocktail, various panini sandwiches and baby spinach salad.

"A man of many talents," she said, leaning back on a cushioned bench and crossing her bare feet at the ankles. She'd chosen a gold chain to complement red toenail polish and a lavender skirt with a slit running along her leg. She'd discarded her light coat in order to reveal a matching long-sleeved Lycra shirt, one which fit every curve with near-sheer willingness. "I had no idea you cooked or played Popeye."

He finished tying off a sail, then filled a plate for her. "One out of two ain't bad. But there's a lot about me you don't know."

Smackdown. She curled her legs beneath her, took a sip of wine to fill the silence. Then, "You don't go near a kitchen?"

"Not unless I'm forced to." He handed her the food. "I've got a good corner grocery near my place."

She accepted the loaded plate, trying hard to still the slight tremble of her hand. He stood over her, so powerful with his shoulders blocking the moonlight, their width covered by a dark T-shirt. Jeans completed his uniform, casting him in the role of a bad guy— stubbled, troubled and misunderstood.

Today, when he'd showed up at the photo shoot, she'd been shaking inside, too. She'd planted her hands on her hips, hoping to anchor herself, to regain some semblance of control.

Now, as he stepped closer to her, her skin tightened, extra sensitive under the sticky assault of marine air.

She set the plate on the bench beside her while he returned to the other side and piled food onto his own.

She caught her breath, half-relieved by the space he'd created.

Calm down, Fi, she thought. If you can't get a handle on yourself, the bet's dust.

"You know why I'm here?" she asked, her tone light and playful.

His shadowed profile—or maybe it was his deep voice—revealed a grin. "To get laid."

She drew back a little. But it was true, wasn't it? She wasn't in this for anything more. "Partly."

"You've got motivations beyond sex?" He stood again, came to sit beside her.

The shivers started up again. God, she hoped they wouldn't claim her voice. "In spite of this seductive setup, there's nothing beyond orgasm for me tonight."

"That's just fine. I'm a very patient man."

His words rolled over her, and her nipples contracted, braless, nudging her top. Inspired, she repositioned herself so that he'd have full view of her breasts, which she knew were completely visible under her formfitting, filmy top.

Hey, if he could try to up the stakes with a sexy dinner, she could play by the same rules.

And it worked. His gaze settled on her chest, caressed it. She took another sip of wine, and the warmth flowed downward, pooling low in her belly.

She breathed deeply, chasing away the funny feeling.

"I'm here," she said, "because I'm going to win."

He reached out, ran a thumb over a crested nipple. Fiona gasped, then moaned, her free hand instinctively seeking his fingers, brushing over them.

He continued rubbing. "Aren't you being premature?"

The boat bobbed with extra vigor, and she suddenly felt dizzy.

In spite of the dangerous spasms of yearning that speared through her, Fiona gathered all her strength, taking her hand from his, trying to wear a serenely composed facade while moving with his every stroke.

"I've got all the confidence in the world," she said, schooling the breathiness out of her tone. "It's not about the prize, you know."

"The Caribbean isn't good enough for you?"

"Oh, no." She bit her lip, then recovered as he cupped underneath her breast, kneading it. "My victory will be more symbolic."

He didn't say anything, just watched her, probably waiting for her to break open, allowing him inside where he didn't belong.

Not in her brain, anyway.

"It's a triumph for all women," she said, smiling at him with sleepy emphasis.

A grin slanted over his mouth, his hand trailing down her ribs, thumb etching the line of her inner thigh. Then he stood, going to the opposite side of the boat, sitting on the edge of it while digging into his food with relish.

Excuse me? Here she was, her heart pounding

through her body like it was a bass drum, and he'd left her?

So that's how it'd be, huh? She'd show him what it was like to be left in the lurch.

Lurch. The boat nodded, and Fiona closed her eyes.

Recovering, she thought that now it was really about winning, toying with him as he was with her. She only wished she'd had this same opportunity with Ted, before he'd run off with Crissy Banks.

Her best friend.

Oh, if she could've wrapped Ted around her little finger and peeled him off with deliberate payback, she would've. Would've teased him to the point of suffering. Would've let him know what he would miss for the rest of his life.

Now, if she could stay strong with Mac...

She stopped, exhaling, head beginning to ache. This was wrong, using him as a substitute for her resentment.

It was only about sex. It had been for years.

Fiona calmed herself, dipping a piece of shrimp into the cocktail sauce. Even if she'd lost her appetite, she couldn't help licking off the spicy concoction when Mac glanced over. Couldn't help laving the curve of the meat, hinting at what she'd be doing to him later.

His response was somewhere between a chuckle and a grunt. "You're a competitor, all right."

"Hey. Tit for tat. You'll be difficult, I'll be more difficult. I was raised to win."

"Whoa. Do we want to go there?"

She made a show of devouring the shrimp, then

prepared another one. "Family talk is fine. Likes, dislikes—okay by me. Past relationships—definitely off-limits."

"Agreed." He drained his own wine, returned his attention to eating. "You a California girl?"

What an appetite the man had. It was fitting, though, judging by his stamina in other areas.

She pretended not to notice. "I moved here for college."

"And you've got siblings. That explains your competitive nature."

"Well read, Mac." She sucked on a strawberry until he glanced away, shaking his head. Ha ha... Oooo, the waves were getting choppy. "Three brothers. The oldest ones are twins. Hellraisers, those guys, both sporty types. My other older brother is a high school basketball coach."

"You're just one of the boys, aren't you?"

Sometimes she felt like it. In fact, she'd always done her best to be in the boys' clubs at work. That's how a lady succeeded in this business. "I used to play Little League because I wanted to do everything my brothers did. I was a pitcher."

Mac set down his empty plate, leaned a muscled arm on his thigh. "You're kidding."

She delicately set aside her own plate, unable to deal with food any more. "Don't sound so patronizing. I pitched my team to a championship."

Mac held up his hands. "Hey, didn't mean to offend you. My mom would've had a coronary if my sisters played ball."

"My mother died when I was young, so she wasn't around to chastise me."

A swell of emotion washed over her, pressing down on her chest. She cleansed herself of it, knowing this wasn't the time or the place.

Mac paused. "I'm sorry to hear that. I really didn't have a mom, either."

Sean didn't want to talk about this. Didn't want to tell her how the woman known as "mother" had deserted the family and left a mess known as "dad" behind.

Fiona considered him, dark eyes boring into his soul. In that incredibly hot outfit, she resembled a contented cat lounging on a couch, licking its paws with lazy strokes, planning its next move.

Damn, she had him dancing on his last nerve. That's why he'd retreated to this side of the boat. Because he didn't know what he'd do next.

Could she win, not by staying detached, but by effortlessly possessing *him?*

Wouldn't happen.

"But," he said, stretching up to a stance, tucking his hands under his arms to keep everything inside, "I do have two pain-in-the-butt sisters. Both are married, of course and, in their tormented state of matrimony, both want to see me tie the knot, too."

"Misery does love company."

He hadn't been joking about the torment. Katie and Colleen constantly complained about their husbands, reaffirming Sean's belief that love wasn't worth it.

His first clue had come in the form of his mom.

Echoing his body language, Fiona unsteadily got to her bare feet, her ankle bracelet shining in the lantern light. Her dress absorbed the glow, revealing the dark centers of her breasts, the hint of a caressable stomach, her belly button.

Sean's muscles clenched, imprisoning him.

He fought to be released. "Wait," he said. "Don't move."

She didn't, except for the fingers that were plucking the sides of her skirt. Nerves? He wished. Her anxiety meant something more than pure lust was happening, and that would lead to victory for him.

He brushed aside the curiosity, knowing anything beyond sex wasn't in the plan.

"What?" A wobbly laugh rode the end of her question.

He stared a moment longer, consuming her. "I'm putting you in my mental scrapbook."

"Oh." She exhaled, looked away, put a hand on her tummy. "Are you done now?"

"You don't like to be looked at?" He never would have expected this from a beautiful woman like Fiona.

Her slight smile made him forget every other image in the bulging memory tome of his brain. Women: petite, long-limbed, brunette, blond, redheaded... They were all there, asking him what they'd done wrong.

"Are you through?" she asked, her grin wobbling.

He pushed aside the other women, their questions. "You're eager."

Fiona reached for the cabin, slumping against it.

''Looking a little pale there. You okay?'' he asked.

''I think I'm a bit seasick,'' she said, rubbing a hand over her temple.

''Do you need help?''

She shook her head. ''Sorry about the bad timing, but I'm not feeling well right now. Maybe it was the motion of the ocean.''

As she closed her eyes and held her stomach, Sean realized she wasn't putting on a show. Looks like he'd lost tonight's battle.

But definitely not the war.

FORGET THE WAR.

Sean couldn't get back to work because he was too concerned about Fiona. Last night, she'd gotten sick. Yeah. Throwing-up-over-the-side-of-the-boat sick.

He'd held back her hair and smoothed a hand over her spine as she'd cleared her stomach, apologizing the whole time.

''I hate having you see me like this,'' she'd said, voice wavering.

Sure, she'd been at her worst but in a weird way, Sean hadn't minded so much. She'd clung to him, not in passion, but in a different kind of need. He'd been around to help and it felt kind of decent.

Even as he'd motored the boat to shore and driven her back home, catching a taxi to return to his place, Sean hadn't minded the night's outcome.

He shook himself to the present and caught himself smiling like a dope. What the hell?

Getting out of his chair, he paced to the window

which showcased the Boulevard. Upscale clothing
stores and talent agency offices stretched down the
pavement. Tourists and locals bustled down the sidewalks.

He barely saw them. All that mattered was Fiona.
Erudite, saucy, completely compatible with his needs
in bed. When he could get her there.

He'd never met a woman like her before, and probably never would again. Maybe he should get out of
their affair now, before he really lost it.

If he hadn't already.

Oh. Hell, no. He wasn't capable of feeling. Didn't
want to be. Would never be.

His father had taught him well. Not that Jimmy
McIntyre had made it a point to show his son how
much love hurt. In fact, the man had tried to hide it
for a while.

After Mom had left because of all those arguments
about money and other things Sean didn't grasp, his
dad had continued with life for a while—marching
into his Chicago law firm on a daily basis with his
morning cup of coffee in hand, making sure Sean and
his sisters were well-provided for. But one day, when
Sean had ditched high school early, he'd found out
that Jimmy Mac had been living a lie.

He'd discovered his father at twelve noon, sitting in
a kitchen chair near a window that overlooked the
driveway, dressed in his business suit, obviously
watching for Mom. He'd avoided all questions and,
when Sean had asked one of his father's business as-

sociates what was going on, the man had told him that Jimmy had been fired from the firm a few weeks ago.

From that point on, Sean and his sisters had done their best to run the household, living off their father's unemployment while it lasted. Then they'd moved on to his sister's paychecks for the next few years until they married their way out of the household.

Sean had eventually gone to a local college where he could keep an eye on his father, who continued to wait for Mom, no matter how many years passed. His time in front of the window decreased, but the look in his eyes never changed. In his mind, he was obviously still watching for her.

Now, years later, Sean continued to send money home while Katie and Colleen took turns checking on Dad. Sean visited once in a while, but he couldn't stand to see his father still waiting in front of that window.

He backed away from his own view, shaken. There was work to do. Lots of it.

"Sean?" asked a voice through his speakerphone. Carly, his trusty assistant.

He pressed the answer button. "Yeah?"

"Fiona Cruz wants to know if you're available."

His stomach jumped. She'd come to work? "Tell her to get in line."

"Um..." Pause. "Okay."

He shouldn't have growled at Carly. The poor girl had nothing to do with his thwarted sex drive.

He left his office and passed Carly at her desk on his way down the hall to Fiona's, nodding to the assistant. Note: Get the woman some flowers to tell her how much he appreciated her hard work, then their slate would be clean again.

As he walked the hall, he caught the aroma of lunch: hot dogs, burritos, hamburgers. Heart attack food. Come to think of it, he needed a meal himself. Might as well encourage the inevitable.

When he drew up to Fiona's office, he stopped short.

There she was, one long, black-stockinged leg thrown over the other, body encased in a deep purple suit with gypsy ruffles. The only reminder of last night's tummy troubles was a trace of white tinting her skin. Was she trying to ignore the weakness she'd shown?

A healthy lunch—salad, chilled water and fish tacos—waited on the opposite side of her desk. And she was reading something, hardly bothering to hide the book cover.

The Sensuous Woman, by "J."

"You've clearly recovered," he said.

"Fit as a fiddle." She stretched a little, her supple body reminding him of what he'd missed out on.

That's okay. He could contain himself. "I thought you'd stay home today."

She pulled an unconcerned face. "Not to worry. I'm a trouper." She smiled a little. "Thanks for...well, helping me out."

"All in a night's work."

She hesitated, as if wanting to say something else.

But instead, she set down *The Sensuous Woman,* gave it a gentle pat.

Sean shook his head, then took a chair.

"This is nice," Fiona said, tearing off a slice of flour tortilla and putting it in her mouth. She squinched her face. "Lunching with you. Braving the corporate atmosphere."

He watched her chew with that disgusted expression on her face. "What happened to 'let's keep sex out of the office'?"

"I am."

He grabbed a taco, decided he might as well eat. "Come on. You're making damned sure I know you're reading that book."

"Oh. *That.*"

"You're not going to break me down, no matter what you have up your..." He grinned. "Sleeve."

"I've got more than you bargained for." She ran her fingers over the book's nondescript cover. "When I was about twelve, I found a drawer in our living room that had all these naughty novels in it. All I remember now was *Mandingo* and this one."

"Mandingo?" He polished off the first taco.

"Long story. Anyway, I used to sneak into the living room and pretend to be listening to the stereo while I was really reading." She tilted her head, lifting one eyebrow. "And learning."

"Twelve years old?"

"Don't worry. I didn't start putting my knowledge into practice until college. But we're not going there, remember?"

"Especially here."

"Exactly."

Forget past relationships. Were they even supposed to be talking about dirty books? Sean definitely didn't want to ask. This was too entertaining. Besides, he could handle the erotic prodding.

Really.

"Where was I?" She tapped a red nail against her lips, drawing his attention to them.

Lips. The ones he hadn't felt since...

"The book," he choked out.

"Right. When you came in the office, I was just reading about a little something called The Butterfly Flick."

Oh, damn.

"Stop," he said.

"I'm discussing literature with you over lunch."

"Fiona..."

She sent a wicked grin at him. "Just reminding you that I'm in charge, Charles."

Sean lifted a finger to make another point. Something about her not being the one who was driving this revved-up bus to hard-on-ville, but his cell phone rang before he had the chance to say it.

He glanced at her, and she gave him an unconcerned shrug. Go for it.

After unholstering the phone, he answered. "McIntyre, here."

"It's Lakota."

Great. He shot a look to Fiona, and she knew who

it was right away. She leaned forward, narrowing her eyes.

"What can I do for you?" he asked, raising a wry brow at his co-worker.

She smiled in appreciation, nodding at his double talk.

"Well…" Lakota hesitated, and he knew this wasn't going to be good. "I was wondering if we could meet today. You know. Right now, actually. To plan strategy."

Good God. Did Lakota think she was his only client? "Know what? I can put your manager through to Carly, and she can make an appointment. I'm swamped today with the work I should've been doing yesterday. You know, when you called me to the photo shoot."

"Oh, that." Another pause. "Um…"

Fiona's phone rang, and she picked up. "Hello?"

Lakota spoke. "I'd really like to talk to you. Show my appreciation for all the work you've done. You deserve a bonus for putting up with me."

Fiona leaned back in her chair, gesturing toward her phone while she listened to her caller. Clearly it was either Lincoln or his manager.

"What's going on?" Sean asked Lakota.

"All right. Lincoln Castle and I got into a bit of a tiff at a restaurant near the studio."

"And…?"

"And a columnist for Soap Serial Online was there. Karen Carlisle."

Sean cursed. "When is this crap going to stop, Lakota?"

"It was a long day and…" She started to cry.

Cry?

Why couldn't she bother her manager with this garbage?

"Calm down," he said, gentling his tone.

"I hate Lincoln Castle. Do you know what it's like having to work with him?"

As she bitched further, Sean glanced at Fiona, but she'd gotten out of her chair, all business, and was pacing the carpet. He grabbed a pen from her desk, a piece of paper. Then he wrote, "We'll talk about literature later. Lots to work out."

With a burst of resigned frustration, he got out of the chair, leaving the rest of his lunch. Fiona turned around, and he pointed to the note.

She lifted her hand at him in a lazy goodbye, then returned to her call.

Sean stood there for a moment, emptiness lining the pit of his stomach.

Lakota's voice intensified. "So what should I do?"

He turned to go, chancing one last glance at Fiona, who still had her back to him. Dismissed.

As he made his way through the halls, back to an office filled with work he'd have to ignore until he returned tonight, he clutched the phone, almost to the point of throttling it.

"Let me contact Karen Carlisle while I drive to meet you. We're going to talk this out. Once and for all."

"Thanks, Sean. You're the best, and I won't forget this."

He hoped she wouldn't. If she became the star he thought she could be, her devotion would amount to his comeback.

She continued. "Meet me at Moulin Rouge Lingerie on Abbot Kinney Boulevard in Venice. I'm on my way."

And he was, too, even though he'd left Fiona and last night's strange bond behind.

6

LAKOTA STOOD in front of the cute cottage that housed Moulin Rouge Lingerie, knowing she'd messed up yet again.

What was it about Lincoln that drove her nuts? The fact that he'd so quickly gotten back into the good graces of the soap fans while she'd had to work her butt off to merely garner their attention? The way everyone on the set seemed to love him and cater to him, even though he hadn't earned it yet?

Or maybe she was so upset with him because she still had a tender spot in her heart for the guy.

There. She'd admitted it. She'd never gotten over Lincoln. Even after that horrific breakup, where she'd accused him of stepping out on her and he'd denied it, she still adored him.

Why? It wasn't logical, wasn't smart.

Sean McIntyre pulled into a curbed parking space in his timeworn gray Jeep. Thank goodness he was here. She could always count on her publicist, even more than her co-workers and friends, manager, agent, personal assistant, makeup artist...

Okay. So maybe he looked a little put out.

"Hey," she said, smiling brightly, peeking out at

him from underneath the baseball cap she used as camouflage.

He didn't answer, just ambled toward her, features etched in bristled weariness.

A little nervous now that he was actually here—boy, had she been putting him through the wringer—Lakota started to climb the steps that led into the shop.

"Thanks for meeting me."

"I'm not going in there." Sean rested one hand on his holstered cell phone, immovable.

Lakota stuck out her bottom lip in a pout. It didn't work with Sean, of course. "They've got the cutest selection. Indulge me? Please?"

With a disbelieving chuff, he walked away from her. Lakota hopped off the stairs, intent on catching up to his long stride.

"I talked to Karen Carlisle on the way over," he said. "She's not going to report your spat with Lincoln."

"Oh. That's good news. Isn't it? I mean, he and I are supposed to adore each other and—"

"—You're giving her a tour of your house next week. You'll have tea on the balcony and reveal all the sweet dreams that dance around in your head. You'll tell her how much you respect and *adore* your co-star."

Lakota stopped in her steps, but Sean kept going.

"Wait!"

"I'm not licking your boots, Lakota."

She used her sweetheart voice. "But I pay you to do that."

This time he did halt. Even though he wore a starkly chic Armani suit, he still seemed scruffy around the edges. A wild card.

He held up a finger, leaned toward her. Ten feet away, and she shrank back anyway.

"There comes a point in a man's life where he doesn't give a shit anymore." The finger came down, and he should've seemed less intimidating. But he wasn't. Not with that bar-brawl gaze he was leveling at her.

"I've reached my limit," he said, resuming his unhurried gait. "At least for today."

Had he just told her off? Ever since months ago, when Lakota had started inching up the fan marketing polls and getting guest spots on prime time, no one had talked to her like this. Could PR people do that? She'd never had her own rep before, and *Flamingo Beach*'s publicist was too busy to sass her.

Maybe Sean McIntyre really didn't care about kissing his clients' butts. She'd heard about his fire-in-the-belly ambition from another actress and, in an effort to spin herself into a starring nighttime role soon, she'd seized the opportunity to work with him.

Thank goodness. With his guidance, her numbers had exploded, allowing her to recently renegotiate for an unbelievably lucrative contract. Prime time was around the corner. Just as it'd once been for Linc.

Her manager and agent told her that a hungry, ambitious man like McIntyre would come cheaper than the rest, that he'd work his tush off for her in order to get back on top. And he did work like a madman. But she'd never expected to feel so comfortable with him—like she was the little sister and he was the big brother who gave all her prom dates the third degree.

He was a keeper, all right.

Sean was about a block away now, and he hadn't backtracked. Left her behind, had he?

Hmm. Maybe she *was* only twenty-two, pretty much a kid in many ways. But couldn't he take her seriously?

Lakota speed-walked after him, taking care to appear that she wasn't exerting herself in the least. As she closed the distance, two teenage girls did a double take at her. She chanced a quick smile at them then ducked under the bill of her hat.

Maybe Sean had superhero senses, because he glanced over his shoulder, hardly surprised she'd run after him.

"You left me standing there," she said.

"I suppose I did."

Out of the corner of her eye, Lakota caught sight of the teenagers, who were huddled together, whispering.

Sean nodded approvingly. "Recognition. Good. But I'm surprised they know it's you."

"Why?" Usually, she loved to chat with her fans. But she wanted to be herself right now—not Rita Wilde, her soap character. Lakota started speed walking in the other direction.

Sean easily kept up. "It's that sophisticated stage makeup you wear on the show. Without it, you look about seven years younger. And, anyway, who'd expect *Flamingo Beach* vixen Rita Wilde to be walking around in a flannel shirt and jeans?''

Lakota felt herself blush. Most actresses wore full makeup and a snazzy wardrobe in public. Not her. ''Once I take off the slinky dresses and get back into my street clothes, I leave the soap behind. Just like I thought I'd left Lincoln.''

''Ah.''

He didn't say anything more, and she didn't know if she wanted to, either. Would he laugh himself silly if he knew she still carried a torch for Linc?

Well, she wouldn't tell him, that was for sure. Nobody needed to know about that particular embarrassment. Their time together had been brief—an emotion-packed two months—but it'd marked her forever.

They passed Abbot Kinney's funky boutiques, art galleries, neon green fliers taped to the lampposts announcing a clean needle program for drug users. L.A. rocked.

A particularly attractive vintage shop caught Lakota's eye, and she tugged on Sean's sleeve to guide him inside.

''I thought you wanted to talk game plans, not piddle around,'' he said, crusty as ever.

''Admit it. You're crazy about me, just like siblings in the back seat of a car during the family trip. Sure, you want to kill me right now, but if I really did end up getting hurt, you'd be all torn apart.''

Lakota finished with one of her perky grins. A real one.

He relented, and once inside the vintage shop, Sean,

seemingly bored, muttered something beneath his breath and got busy lounging next to a wicker basket overflowing with faded pictures. She poked through the lot of them, snapshots of more interesting lives than hers. Family vacations, children with slicked-back hair and lacy collars smiling into the camera.

She grabbed one. A girl from the sixties, wearing a pageboy, a graduation gown and a dazzling smile. She stood between her parents, holding a diploma.

Flashing it to Sean, she said, "Might as well get a life, right?" Her voice cracked.

Concern cocked his brow. "You okay?"

"Oh, sure." Lakota impulsively grabbed a pair of cranberry suede boots. Too big, but maybe she could stuff the toes with newspaper. Then she fingered some neckties dangling from a hanger, choosing a vivid pea-cock-blue one. She could be so Annie Hall.

She unloaded the items on a glass-topped counter, and the owner smiled at her from under his salt-and-pepper mustache. When she glanced back down, the photo consumed her focus.

A family. A mom and dad who cared, who were proud of their diploma girl.

Lakota's midwestern mom had always said she was an idiot. Pretty, but how far was that going to get you? Her father... Let's just say he'd never been in the picture. Any picture.

Agitated, she proceeded to flit around the shop. Lakota could feel Sean watching her while she inspected brooches, bridesmaid dresses, pillbox hats and a shiny

Boba Fett lunchbox. In a dusty corner, she even found a music box that played the theme from *Love Story*.

Music boxes.

She swallowed, cradled it to her chest with the other purchases.

When she returned to the counter, she caught Sean staring at a 40s movie star nightgown, his gaze naked with repressed fire.

"Buy it for her," she said, wiggling her eyebrows.

Sean's jaw unclenched in apparent surprise.

Lakota turned to the owner, who was standing by patiently, adding up her purchases. "Men. They think girls have no clue."

The clerk didn't say anything. Maybe he knew better than to get into these sorts of conversations.

"And what is it you've figured out?" Sean asked, slightly less annoyed than fifteen minutes ago, thank goodness.

Lakota inspected the chokers hanging on a rack in front of her. "You think we don't know what's going on inside your heads, but it's painfully obvious."

"Hate to tell you, but a lot of our thoughts center around one thing."

"I know." The backs of her eyelids pricked, signaling the start of tears she'd already cried. "Unfortunately, sometimes one woman isn't enough for a guy."

Sean came up behind her, and she immediately felt safer, more comfortable. Protected.

"This is about Lincoln, isn't it?"

"I can't stand him. You know, I was thinking, can

you spin some bad publicity his way? He's making me look like a viper.''

Shut up, Lakota, she thought. *You don't really mean it.*

Sean didn't say anything, probably because he was thinking she was doing a good job of ruining her image on her own.

Instead, Lakota heaved out a breath, moisture stinging one corner of an eye as she turned to him. ''I'm so in love with him, and there's no chance he's ever going to feel the same. To top it off, I'm being such a jerk about it.''

At first, Sean made a you-got-that-right expression, but it turned into a look of pity instead.

See? Her publicist was more than worth what she paid him.

She sniffed, shrugging. ''I suppose I want to put the screws to him before he puts them to me this time.''

''What did he do wrong?''

A chopped laugh, full of regret. ''I thought he was cheating, even though I didn't have any evidence. I don't know. I was a nobody, and he was... God. Lincoln Castle, the soap star. It's hard to live with a guy who's the fantasy of so many women. He could have his pick.''

''But he wanted you.''

''Hard to believe.'' That stubborn tear finally welled, tumbled down her cheek. She swiped at it, bucking up to show that Lincoln didn't affect her. ''Have you ever felt this way? Crummy and ecstatic to be around a certain person, all at the same time?''

An antique clock ticked on the wall behind Sean. Then, "Sometimes we make it harder than it needs to be, I suppose."

The shopkeeper had sneaked away to the other side of the store, leaving them alone. Embarrassment swallowed her up. Why couldn't she have kept this angst to herself instead of letting it all out? She'd also let fly today in the restaurant, and it hadn't been pretty.

Sean had shoved his hands in his pockets, glancing away from her. Hard as a profile on Mount Rushmore, wasn't he?

"Once," he said, voice low, barely there, "I was with a woman. I couldn't think of anything but her, during work, when I got home...always. Neither of us was looking for anything serious, so we messed around, kidded each other. Made a bet that she wouldn't get emotionally involved during the course of our affair."

"Did she?"

"No." Sean turned his back on her, ran a hand over a pile of outdated records. Lakota noticed that his fingers were curled, as if wanting to tear at something.

"How could you do that?" she asked. "Make a bet about love?"

"Not love."

She couldn't see his face, but his voice told her more than he'd probably wanted to reveal.

Sean tensed up, left the shop.

Lakota watched him go, frowning. There was a glitch in his story, something out of place, as if...

Her own problems shoved to the back of her mind,

she grabbed the nightie he'd been ogling. It flowed like olive oil over her fingers, the amber color rich and heavy.

"Excuse me?" she said to the shopkeeper. "Will you ring this up, too, please?"

Five minutes later, lingerie hidden in her bag and a devious spring in her step, she emerged from the store. She headed toward her favorite shop, a boutique that sold flower essences. Keeping his distance, Sean loitered while the assistant used a pendulum to lead them to the proper brandy/water potions, much like one would use a divining rod to locate water. Lakota had requested something to help with her career, and she walked out with three bottles that would do just that if taken internally two times a day.

"You believe in this?" he asked.

"Absolutely. Mind over matter. Oh!" She took his hand, walked him across the mellow street to another quaint cottage. This one had Perfumery written on a sign in the yard. "I'm out of my fragrance."

"Order it online."

"It's personalized. They mix it for me."

"You have your own perfume?" His mind really wasn't on the question or the shopping. He'd felt sorry for Lakota, with her scrubbed face and tomboy baseball cap. Felt sorry enough to talk where he shouldn't have been talking.

That damned nightgown had softened him up. He'd pictured Fiona underneath the silk. Curves lit by warm, licking flame, his fingers slipping the material up, over her body.

He fisted his hands.

"Just come in," said Lakota. "They've got a lounge, and we'll have a drink. Then we can get down to business. And..." She shook her massive purchase bag. "I've got something for you."

"Don't tell me."

She opened the top, giving him a peek of smooth silk. "We can talk advice, if you want. I owe you."

Advice? Who was this kid to be offering it?

She gave a little hop of excitement, and he couldn't deny her the satisfaction of giving him a present. Hell, maybe he would end up giving the gown to Fiona, but without the gift wrap of emotion.

Why not?

Sean held out his arm, and Lakota took it. Together, they walked up the cottage stairs.

BACK AT Stellar Public Relations, Fiona was still on the phone. This time, instead of Linc's manager, she was talking with the man himself.

She'd already chastised him for the restaurant argument with Lakota, and Mac's assistant had told her that he'd taken care of Karen Carlisle on his end. For her part, Fiona had spent about a half hour guaranteeing the online reporter exclusive interviews with Lincoln for the next couple of months.

Bribery, the foundation of the entertainment business. But they called it "leverage."

Fiona's stomach coiled and she reached for a water bottle on her desk, finding only the crushed remains of three other containers. Last night hadn't only left her dehydrated, it'd caused her to go back to square one with Mac. Frustration, anyone?

"Lincoln," she said into the phone, "I'm about to send you to military school, you know. You need some discipline."

"I can't help myself." He sounded agitated, and she hoped he didn't have any liquor handy. "When I get around Lakota, my circuits go haywire."

"Self-accountability. Remember that phrase?"

"Yeah, I do. From months of rehab."

"Good boy." She couldn't help the fondness from overwhelming her tone. "If I didn't know any better, I'd say you were still in love with Lakota, and that's why you can't contain yourself."

Pure, utter silence.

"Oh, no."

"Fi, don't sound so disappointed. It's being near her again that's doing me in."

She remembered when Lincoln had first started seeing Lakota a year ago. How they'd gone to restaurants and nuzzled in the corner booths, so consumed with each other that they'd shut the places down without knowing how much time had passed. She remembered when the relationship had exploded—not burned out. He'd spent seven nights on Fiona's couch, not wanting to go home to an empty bed.

Then the real trouble had started. He'd just begun working on his prime-time show—acting by day, carousing in the bars by night, picking up the random women who reminded him of Lakota. Crashing his motorcycle into a guardrail on the 405 Freeway one foggy evening, his blood alcohol level at twice the legal limit.

The show had fired him then, killing off his character after only three months.

"I've grown up," he said, clearly knowing what she was thinking.

"I hope so, Linc. God, I really hope so."

"Are you mad at me?"

The question took her aback. "For what?"

"Nothing."

The one word said it all. "What, you think I'm jealous because you're in the throes of love and I'm... not?"

Why had she hesitated? What she had going with Mac had nothing to do with tender declarations of forever, even after the way he'd held her head last night.

Great, she thought. Barfing, the language of modern romance.

Linc sighed. "You could be happy. If you didn't believe you'd had your moment with Ted and it'll never happen again, you could—"

"—What I had with Ted can hardly be described in Shakespearean sonnets. It'd take something more like a tragedy to fill in those blanks."

"Ted was a loser. I've told you that a million times."

So why didn't she believe it? "I thought I was the person who lost in that scenario," she said softly.

Images assaulted her: Ted holding her hand while they watched the Dodgers playing the Padres, the two of them feeding each other hot pretzels and snuggling throughout the game. Ted taking her for a ride to rural Ramona, just outside of San Diego, where he'd asked her if she could imagine living with him on a small ranch, where he'd slipped the ring onto her finger. Ted holding her after they'd made love behind a cove of rocks on a blanket at the beach, counting the stars with her, making her wish on each one. Ted calling her in a hotel room one night to say that he and Crissy had gone to Vegas during one of Fiona's many business trips.

That they'd gotten married.

She'd never seen it coming, him and Crissy. She'd been putting in too many hours at her new publicist's job. But she should have. Even Linc had commented about how Crissy looked at Ted. How Ted always affectionately kidded Crissy about how she'd managed to retain her small-town innocence, even in L.A.

God, she'd never be that stupid again. Would never open herself up to that sort of anguish.

"Fiona?" Linc, probably thinking she'd jumped out the high-rise window.

"I'm here." She blindly shuffled through some papers on her desk.

"You'll find the one," he said.

Fiona forced a light laugh. "Spoken like a man in love."

"Right. How am I going to handle this with Lakota?"

"Be careful," she said. She put all those meaningless papers to the side of her desk. "Just..."

"Watch out. I know." He chuckled. "Will do."

They blabbed a few more minutes, then said their goodbyes. As the sun set over Wilshire Boulevard, Fiona leaned back in her chair, the light from the window listing over her blank walls. She hadn't decorated yet. Hadn't had the time. But she would soon.

That's what she always said.

An hour could've passed. Maybe two. Whatever the case, most everyone had gone home. It was dark when Mac's assistant tapped on Fiona's door, a plain box in hand.

"Fiona? Sean asked me to run this down the hall to you."

Her pulse skittered. "He's in his office?"

"Working like a demon, playing catch-up." Carly set the box on Fiona's desk. "I think this has something to do with the whole *Flamingo Beach* thing."

Business. Of course. "Thank you," she said as Carly left, waving good-night.

The minute the assistant disappeared, Fiona attacked the delivery, peeking under the lid before throwing it away altogether.

She sucked in a breath at the sight of the gown. Then she darted over to her office door, closing it. Back to the lovely piece of work.

It reminded her of a gin joint, an evening of Cotton Club seduction. If she put it on, would the material curl around her skin like smoke dancing from the tip of a lit cigarette?

Oh, Mac.

Mac. Damn him. This wasn't playing fair.

She picked up her phone, rang his extension.

"Sean McIntyre."

Again, with the accelerated pulse, the tingles and anticipation. "What's this all about?"

She could hear him switch off the speakerphone, and his tone lowered to a graveled drag. "You like it?"

She loved it. Loved all pretty things, even if she had pitched a no-hitter when she was ten years old. "It's very sweet of you, but what's it for?"

"Tonight."

Tonight, tonight...

Nuh-uh.

She mewed into the phone. "Let me check my social calendar. Oh, now, I don't see you penciled in."

"Then get to penciling."

"This has to be against the rules."

She could picture him leaning back in his seat, muscles rippling up his long body.

"What rules?" he asked.

What rules, indeed? "All right. Your place again. Say, eleven?"

Always his place. Always in control of when she left.

"As long as I can sleep in on my Saturday morning," he said. "But I am coming into the office tomorrow."

"Glutton. And don't worry. I won't inconvenience you by overstaying my welcome."

Neither of them said anything, and Fiona took that as approval on his end. The silence stung.

She lowered her tone to a whisper, ignoring the slight. "Be ready for my mouth all over your body."

He gave a strangled moan. Good, back in the driver's seat.

When she hung up, she dropped the phone.

What was this?

She stared at the handle, at her trembling hand.

Nerves. Excitement. That's all.

She put the piece back in its cradle, taking a deep breath.

Mental foreplay. Nothing more.

That's what she kept telling herself as she took the back way out of the office.

7

MARINA DEL REY was an upscale area where the houses piled on top of themselves as they perched on the banks of the boat-lined bay. Lincoln cut his Harley's engine as he drove onto a quiet street. At 10:30 p.m., it was rude to shatter the peace with his growling machine, and the last thing he wanted to do was draw attention to himself.

Except in the eyes of one person.

Lakota lived by the canal in a Venetian-inspired two-story home. He secured his bike below her dark window, took out the flashlight.

His thumb rested on the activation switch. No turning back if he flicked it forward.

What was he doing here? His impulsiveness had overstepped its bounds this time, but he couldn't sleep, knowing he'd fallen for her again. Knowing he'd fought with her today.

Did he want to revisit all the pain? The keening hollowness of knowing he'd failed her during their first go-around? Did he want the temper, the stubborn ambition that went with Lakota?

He beat the flashlight against his leg. Why was he here anyway?

When he glanced toward her balcony, a curtain rustled through the open French doors. It was like she stood right next to him—orange-blossom perfume mixed with the ocean breeze.

Not long ago, she'd rested her head against his chest after making love. Content in the afterglow, he'd close his eyes, taking on the weight of her slight body, wrapping his arms around her like knotted ropes, burying his nose in her hair, drawing her into him. Making them one person.

God, he wanted her back. Linc aimed the light at her window, turned it on, played the beam over the misty curtains, realizing it probably wouldn't be enough to attract her attention.

Well, it'd been a good idea when he'd hopped on his Harley.

"Lakota," he said in a harsh stage whisper.

No answer. Well, maybe he'd have to get practical rather than romantic. He reached into his bomber jacket pocket, took out his cell phone, speed-dialed her. He'd never removed her number.

One ring. Two rings. Breathe, man, breathe.

She answered on the third. "Yes?" Sleep weighed down her voice.

He didn't know if he was relieved or concerned that she was in bed so early on a Friday night. Where was the Lakota who worked her connections at The Sky Bar? The Viper Room?

Linc didn't say anything, just used a point of light to write her name on the curtains.

Seconds later, she peeked around the material. "Lincoln? Is that you?"

She knew who it was. He shut off the flashlight, waited, but she didn't move. "Come out, Kota."

The sound of a nearby car traveling the streets stretched the awkward moment.

Was she still angry at him?

Linc stepped closer to the balcony, speaking softly into the phone. "I hear Karen Carlisle's going to visit you next week, compliments of your publicist."

"I hear you've got the same punishment."

Odd, how he'd been inside her only months ago, only to be talking to her from a distance right now. Sure, fame isolated him. So did failure, to an even greater degree. But not being able to get close to the woman he still loved...jeez, that's right, *loved*...put him in the middle of a wasteland, made Linc feel like a remnant, a bleached bone stranded in a place no one would ever find him.

"Please come out," he said.

This time, all the contained anguish throttled his voice. And she must've heard it, too, because she did as he asked, slipping around the curtain, revealing a petite, fawn-legged body barely hidden by white babydoll pajamas. She wore her red hair in a ponytail and, even from this distance, he could catch the pale of the moon in her blue eyes.

"Hi," he whispered.

She moved closer, leaning an elbow on the balcony railing in order to fix the phone to her ear. She stood right above him, and he closed his eyes, savoring her.

"I'm sorry about lunch," she said.

He could hear her real voice and the phone voice at the same time. Still, if he hung up, he was afraid he'd lose her, afraid he'd jinx this run of civil interaction.

"I apologize, too," he said, opening his gaze again, gulping at the way the moonlight filtered through her pajamas. The material draped over those small, beautiful breasts—breasts that had filled the cup of his hands, sustaining him.

His palms tingled from the want of her.

"You know," she said, oblivious, "at that restaurant, I was talking extra loudly about your beer belly because I half hoped you'd hear and I'd get a rise out of you." Lakota shook her head. "Isn't that stupid?"

"Stupid? That's something your mother would say. Never me. And you did provoke me into facing off with you, so your grand plan worked."

"Too well. I didn't mean any of it."

"Not the cracks about the extra pounds? Or the bags under my eyes?"

Lakota covered her face with her free hand. "You don't have either. It's just that..."

Say something personal, he thought. *I don't want to be the first one to put myself out there. Not this time.*

The warm night air hung between them. No words. No chances.

So, she wasn't going to take a risk, either. That's the way it was, then. Probably for the best anyway.

Her body angled away from him. "I can't believe we haven't talked since that night."

An opening. *That night.* The breakup. He'd desperately tried to reach her after she'd left their house, but to no avail. That'd led to him trashing his life, ending up in jail, in rehab, back home with the loving family who'd supported him through thick and thin. They'd healed him, encouraged him to go back to what he loved doing.

Acting. In a soap, on TV. Wherever.

"We can hash it all out now." Linc craved one more look, one more glance that would tell him they were done fighting. For good. "If we can manage not to tear each other up."

But, frankly, fighting had been the basis for their passion. His body remembered it all too well: her sweat on his tongue, salty and thirst-inducing. His skin under her fingernails, a piece of him for her to keep.

If they got near each other again, what would happen? Would they make the same mistakes? Was there a chance of having something more?

Just look at me, he thought. *Please.*

She did, and his heart swelled in his throat.

"You know," she said, the phone mouthpiece so close to her mouth that he could imagine her lips brushing against his, "the fans are right to love you again. In our scene today, when you found Rita Wilde on your doorstep, her clothes messed up from that bad date with Forrest Rockridge…"

Great. She wanted to talk business. Okay, fine by him. All he wanted was to make up with her. Couldn't he settle for that?

She continued, watching him. "...God, the way you looked at Rita brought me into the moment. Won me over."

Me. Her.

A sharp intake of breath signaled that she realized her error. Or was it the truth?

What if she wanted him back as much as he wanted her?

He reached up a hand, beckoning, inviting more than just business. "This storyline's going to bring you an Emmy."

"You think so?" She sounded so young, so unsure.

"Come down here."

Take it slowly, Lincoln.

She backed away from the railing. "I'm not sure this is a good idea. Maybe we'd better keep things..."

His hand fell to his side. "You're right. Bad idea. But maybe we could just drive around on the bike, like we used to. Go wherever we want." It didn't matter where they ended up. He only wanted to be with her again.

"And that's all?" she asked, suspicious.

"That's all."

Moving too fast had been their problem before. They'd shoved a lifetime of need and raging love into two months. There hadn't been trust, just desire, cooling their hungers with each other's bodies.

Lakota turned off the phone, stared at him for a moment, then went back inside, shutting the French doors.

Linc did away with his phone, too. Was this a good or bad sign? Had she locked him out? Would Monday at work be a lower circle of hell for him?

A few minutes passed. Then a few more. He'd blown it, pushed too hard, hadn't he? Damn, he should have apologized and gone. Wiped his hands clean and left well enough alone.

Aching, he righted his Harley, prepared to wheel it out of sight. That's when she sprinted through the front door, dressed in jeans and a sweatshirt.

She came to stand next to him, her head barely reaching his shoulder. Her scent made him dizzy with memories, with new opportunities.

"You were leaving without me," she said. "I hate being left behind."

"I thought you weren't coming."

Gravel crackled under the bike's wheels as they began to walk it out of the neighborhood, their stride matching each other's. Why was this so clumsy? Why was it hard to get a sentence out when, once, they'd pillow talked about everything that mattered at the moment?

Away from the houses, he hid the flashlight, took out their helmets, and gave her one. Straddling the bike, he helped her onto the back seat.

"Remember," she said, "take the ride slow." She popped her helmet on her head, settled her hands on his waist, grooving into the natural fit.

He would take it slow, because this time, he wanted to get it right with Lakota.

Lincoln started the engine, revving it to life.

This time, he'd make sure it was about more than sex.

SEAN WISHED she'd hurry up and get here already.

Finally, at twenty after eleven, he opened the door to find Fiona. She was dressed in a long trench coat, the buttons firmly done up, black-fantasy hair spilling over her shoulders.

His house was in near-darkness, lit only by a dim lamp in the corner of the TV room. Eclipsed, she shot him that wicked smile, her lips pulsing with deep red lipstick.

"Hi," she said. "I'm the Sensuous Woman, and I'm here to practice pages 120 through 121 on you."

The Butterfly Flick? Images of what it might be twisted his veins to the point of popping.

Sean leaned against the door frame, pressing his forehead against a fist. Sheer agony. "You're late."

"The better to keep you in the palm of my hand, my dear."

His ran a rough gaze over her, seeking visual fulfillment from under lowered brows. His nostrils flared, detecting the musk of her own excitement under that coat.

Today, in the perfume shop, Lakota had told him five hundred dollars would buy a consultation. She'd begged him, no joke, to let her get him one. So, he'd thought, why not give Fiona perfume *and* the nightgown? He'd have the bet cinched.

The perfumer had asked him a lot of questions.

What food does your woman like? What spices? Music? Flowers? Era?

Whoa. He knew her complexion and hair color, but when it came to anything else, Sean was sorely lacking.

The realization had jolted him. What did he know about this woman he was screwing?

Did he want to know more?

Fiona sauntered into his home. "I've done some math. A little over three weeks to go until I win."

"Why don't you just throw in the trench coat now?"

A sassy smile lit her face as she watched him over her shoulder. "Is that the only way you'll defeat me? By default?"

Maybe. "What do you have under the wrapping there?"

She turned around, slowly undoing the ties. Sean's stomach constricted, rooting him into place.

She slipped the coat off her burnished shoulders, revealing the lacy straps of that nightgown. His penis thumped, keeping track of every second he couldn't breathe.

Damn, if she had him beaten at this point, he was in for a long night.

Good.

"I washed the gown," she said, voice low, sinuous as heat floating over a tropical moon. "Who knows where it's been?"

"More." Sean's button-fly strained against his growing arousal.

"Patience." She laughed, presenting her back again, allowing the coat to trail a few inches down. It whispered against the silk, exposing a delicious back. Tapering down to the swoop of her waist and hips.

She walked toward his room, as if sniffing out where it was.

"Get back here," he said.

She ignored him, holding a figurative match to his self-control.

"Is this your sanctuary?" she asked, disappearing into the yawning darkness of the hallway.

She was entering a forbidden place. Privacy. His domain.

"Fiona, you strike me as a woman who requires something much more exotic than a bed. Get out here."

"No," her voice echoed.

Dammit. Stubborn freakin' woman.

Sean adjusted a cock that had hardened to one side of his pants, then went after her. "What's the big deal?" he asked. "It's where I sleep."

He entered the room, muttering a curse when he saw what she'd found.

Fiona was inspecting a pair of underwear. Lacy. Red. Belonging to some woman he'd met a month ago at Bailey's.

"Yours?" she asked.

"Now they are."

She dropped them into the corner again, where he kept all his souvenirs. Call him an aberration, but there were nights he couldn't rest unless he had a reminder in his hand. Unless he had himself in the other.

That was the price of being alone and staying that way.

"So," she said, running a taunting gaze over him, "accoutrements?"

"The safest sex."

Her eyes went darker, then she walked away from the bras, the magazines, the scarves one woman had used to tie him to the bedposts before she left in the morning, never to return.

Fiona stood in front of him, so close he could feel the heat rolling off her skin, permeating him. Then she eased the coat farther off her body, the material caught by her curves, then traveling down toward the floor.

Imagining her in the nightgown had been one thing, but reality was another. Her nipples puckered against the thin material, and the sleekness rippled down every mound, every valley, kissing her skin, laving her with decadence. As he peered lower, he could discern the hair between her legs as it crinkled the silk, tempting him to reach out, to cup her there, to use his thumb to rub her awake.

"I can't figure you out, Mac." The coat finally hit the carpet with a thump.

He felt numb, warm, stimulated. Ready.

She held something in one of her hands.

As he reached out, finally coasting his fingers over her sex, into the silk-covered crevice, he asked, "What do you have there?"

Already slippery. Already his.

Without answering, she nudged one leg against him, spreading, then leaned back her head, bit her lip. After moving with the thrum of his fingers, she wiggled, balanced herself by hooking one set of fingers over his shoulder, clenching until her nails bit into his skin.

Still silent, except for a stray moan here and there, she held up her other hand, presented a tube of lipstick. Using one thumb, she flicked off the cover, bringing it to her other hand to wind it up.

Red. Eve-apple red.

She locked gazes with him as she applied it, the color sliding over her ever-amused lips, leaving a blaze of naughtiness behind. Finished, she pressed them together, then inserted a finger into her mouth, dragging the digit out with deliberate ease.

Sean's fingers left the warmth of her, and he pressed against her hip, throbbing. "Why are you in my room?"

"I'm not allowed?" She covered the lipstick, then carelessly tossed it in the corner, along with his other souvenirs. "Oh, your fingers felt so good, Mac."

She reached down between them, touched herself. Touched him.

He tried to hold it together, even with her palm cupped over his erection, enflaming it. Still, he didn't want to let her in—not here, not inside him. "Like my room, there're places best kept out of reach."

With casual indifference, Fiona traced her hands upward, unbuttoned his top. "Especially under our circumstances."

She shucked off the material, leaving him bare. His

ceiling fan whipped air over his sensitized skin while her nails dragged down his chest to rest on his stomach.

When she scratched there, his muscles spasmed, making him grit his teeth.

"There's one thing about you," she said. "You always smell so good. Like...I'm not sure what it is, but it flips my skirt."

As she began undoing his jeans, he held her smooth shoulders, memorizing every move she made. He felt himself getting more turned on with every piece of clothing that hit the ground.

"Maybe it's the perfume of other women," he said.

Cruel. But he wanted to see her eyes. If there was any emotion.

She paused, gaze studied, blank. Then she grinned, bent down as she guided his jeans off. He obligingly stepped out of them.

"I'm happy for you," she said, her face hidden by the fall of her hair.

He glanced away again, not wanting to look at her. Bastard.

"Mac?"

She nestled a kiss behind his knee, and he bucked forward with a grunt.

"That didn't pain you, did it now?" she asked, innocent as a frosted slice of virgin snow.

She smoothed her hands over the front of his thighs, her breath moist against his cock as she panted. Her little breaths felt like jabs of fire, scorching him, bringing all the blood thundering to his groin.

"Oh, look at that," she said, low in her throat. "You've got some lipstick behind your knee."

She tickled him there, then tongued the inside of his thigh, and he jerked, the slickness torching him further.

"And there seems to be a strange smudge here." She grazed her bottom teeth over that last kiss, and Sean rocked her closer, needing her so damned much.

Tease. Her hands were on his ass, kneading the twitching muscles, her chin near his ever-expanding hardness. When he glanced downward, the proximity of her red lips made him sweat even more.

She pressed those lips together, then smiled, running her tongue over her teeth. "I've mentioned The Butterfly Flick, haven't I?"

He couldn't say a damned word, wanted only to take her head between his hands and wrap her mouth around his penis, wetting him, suctioning him to a climax.

"Okay, not a talker during foreplay. I can handle that."

"Shut up, Fiona."

"Quiet yourself, Mac. I've got you where I want you."

She rubbed her cheek against his shaft, and he bunched her hair into his fist.

"Back to The Flick." She sighed. "J. prattles on about this little trick. I guess you're supposed to find a real sensitive spot below the base of the penis, wiggle your tongue back and forth and drive a man to the heights."

Dammit, he wanted to scream.

"But I've never tried it before. Where do you think that spot is?"

"I'll show you."

"Mmm." Fiona smoothed the tips of her fingers up the backs of his legs, making the hairs stand on end, making his blood pound and jitter. "I'm feeling kind of shy tonight. I think I'll wait."

"Bitch."

"Bastard."

He laughed, more out of frustration than anything. Out of patience, he led her back to his erection, needing her to alleviate the buildup.

Instead, she stood, shimmying the front of her silk-encased body against his naked one: breasts smoothing over his thighs, his cock, his belly... Then she stood pushing him backward, right into his closet mirror.

It shivered against his back, its cold facade at odds with her moist warmth.

She fastened her lips to his nipple, coating it with slick heat, bringing it to a fevered nub. After she'd sucked it, she leaned her chin on his chest, her nose brushing his jaw.

"Imagine that," she said. "Another lipstick mark for Mac."

He could still feel the ring of her mouth around his nipple, where her lipstick had no doubt branded him. He dug his fingers into her upper arms, ruthless as a swordsman pointing a blade at her throat.

"Is that a sign of possession?"

Her eyes widened. What was that in their depths? Fear? The shadow of a woman who'd gone too far?

She offered a so-what laugh, traced an index finger around his nipple, wiping at the lipstick. She doubled her efforts, trying to erase the mark.

Enough. He captured her mouth with his, devouring her, nipping at the corners, pulling her upper lip into him. Stroking his tongue across her teeth, he plunged farther inside, invading her.

He had her by the elbows, and she tried to pull back, mewling, then fading into him. One of her gown straps slumped onto the side of his hand, and he slipped his fingers beneath it, tugging.

He had her.

But the next instant, he didn't. She pressed against him again, pummeling him against the mirror, the glass quaking in its tracks. He chuckled as the breath left him.

"Stay still," she commanded.

He couldn't. Not anymore. Not with his pulse buffeting his veins. Not with her so near. So far.

Fiona made her way down his torso, leaving a trail of delicate kisses. He could imagine all the lipstick marks, growing fainter with each slick bite, taking ownership of his body. Each kiss palpitated in time to the count of his heartbeat, getting louder, time bombs set to explode.

She reached his penis and, finally, oh, yeah, *finally,* sucked her lips around the tip of it, pulling, taunting. Continuing the torture, she ran her tongue around his head until it was wet with a mixture of his juices and her saliva.

He threaded his fingers through her loose hair, encouraging her. As she took him into her mouth, she swirled her tongue around him, up, down, thoroughly preparing him. Her fingers sought his balls, her knuckles caressing. Seeking farther behind them she caused him to throw back his head until the mirror shuddered again, rattling against his sweat-coated skin, vibrating dangerous heat through his entire body.

Unable to hold back, he came into her, rocketing forward, groaning with the thrusts, the fallout. She held fast, taking him deeper and deeper, nails cutting the backs of his thighs, as he experienced wracking shake after wracking shake.

He couldn't think. Couldn't focus. Could only hold on to her for dear life.

Neither of them moved. Not for a while. They just panted, recovered.

In the relative stillness, she got to her feet. Planting one final kiss on the side of his neck, she gasped against him, finding the throb of his jugular, and singeing the skin with her obvious sense of victory.

"Done," Fiona said, backing away. Watching him with a naughty, hot gaze, she wiped at her mouth.

Sean stretched his arms over his head, keeping a bead on her as she left the room. "Not quite."

"Gimme some food to refuel this fire, and we'll see about that." She turned around, still in her nightgown, still fully armored.

One last sparring tremble seized him from the inside out. One last strain of clenching fulfillment.

He peered at the empty doorway, barely seeing it through his half-closed lids. Barely able to move.

He'd manage the upper hand. Even if it took the rest of the night, he'd get to her.

8

THE SHAKING NEEDED to stop, thought Fiona, as she wandered into the kitchen and headed straight for the refrigerator.

She took a few deep breaths, calming herself, making sure her fingers hadn't turned to butter, before she whipped open the door. A flood of light and coolness claimed her, plastering itself against the stickiness of her skin.

But she still couldn't stop those trembles. The deep belly-jiggering lack of control.

She focused on the food. God, Mac was such a guy. A package of ground beef, way past its due date—so he really *wasn't* a cook. Three six-packs of Corona— better. A mysterious take-out box that she didn't even want to touch. A jar of maraschino cherries with the stems still attached…maybe that meant there was ice cream in the freezer. And a jar of marshmallow cream with the lid half off. She didn't want to venture a guess as to what *that* was all about.

There, see? Now she was calmer. Back to her search.

Fiona wasn't picky when it came to after-sex sustenance. She usually just wanted to get the taste of her partner out of her mouth, to fill up all the untouched places.

She ran her tongue over her lips, tasting salt. *Him.*

"Any specific hankerings?" Mac asked.

Half ignoring him—good game plan, especially since he hadn't put on a stitch of clothing—she left open the fridge and checked the freezer. No ice cream. Drat.

"What do you eat to survive?" she asked.

When he didn't say anything, she turned around to find him shooting a devilish glance at her body.

The sight of him hit her where it counted, all over, including the lacings of her heart. Those long muscled legs, a penis that could only be described as, *"Yow,"* ridged abs, a brawny chest.

And that face. Chisled from something she couldn't name.

She hardened her resolve, gave a soft, "humph" and turned back to the refrigerator, thankful for the distraction. "Man does not live by copulation alone, you know."

"Says who?"

"Oh, would you just get over here and fix me a marshmallow sandwich or something?"

He ambled across the kitchen floor, gunslinger footsteps thudding on the linoleum.

Gun. Slinging.

Fiona heaved out a trembling breath.

He reached over her, chest to back, the hair of his underarm tickling her shoulder. She stifled a moan of yearning, biting her lip instead.

She'd meant what she'd said about him smelling so good. And not in an artificial designer cologne way, either. Mac had something primal about him—earthy, leathery, like chaps or...

"I could whip up some surprise burgers," he said, touching the package of graying meat.

"Try again." She swallowed as he shifted, his "Yow" nestling between the cheeks of her derriere.

"Beer?"

Was he doing this purposely? Trying to prod her, to slip into her open spaces? His penis had slid downward, inside the backs of her thighs, impeded by the nightgown.

Just for good measure, she wiggled, causing him to start, to nip at her shoulder.

"I guess I should get some drink in me," she said, grabbing two Coronas, moving away.

She heard him take something from the fridge, then shut the door.

"Bottle opener?" she asked.

He accessed a drawer, then handed her the device.

Don't look at him, she thought. *You can still escape without damage tonight.*

If she wanted to.

The beer gasped as she opened one, then the other. The sounds were accompanied by a jar top being screwed off, the metal lid gyrating on the counter.

His voice rode over the noise. "Is the beer what you really want?"

"Sure." She turned around, offered one to him.

He took it, leaning against the counter. He'd already

opened the maraschino cherries. Maybe he liked to snack on them? Maybe they gave him a sugar rush?

After she took a step away, creating a space bubble, he chuffed. Took a swig of beer.

Then, he said, "I guess I meant to ask… What do you like to drink? Really like?"

Okay. He was an after-sex talk guy. He didn't seem too keen on the during-sex part.

"Let's see," she said, resting the tip of the bottle against her lips, playing with it. "I adore a nice Moscato Bianco."

"Wine." He took a cherry by its stem, twiddled it between thumb and forefinger. A drop of thick juice fell to the floor.

She paused, glanced up from the splash, then back at him. "Do you have a favorite cocktail?"

"I'm not particular." He took another drink, then set the cherry on the jar's lid. "How about food?"

Fiona crossed her arms over her chest, beer forgotten. "Chocolate. Steak. Potatoes. Why?"

"Just making small talk. Any spices you prefer?"

"Mac." She held herself closer, arming herself. "What's this all about?"

He shrugged. "Ah. Nothing really. We're allowed to talk about this stuff, right?"

Finally, she sipped at her beer, buying time. What was he up to? More unfair techniques to win the bet?

She came up for air, the beverage's cold bitterness quenching her thirst, spinning her head. "I suppose we can chat. But these are weird questions. Even for you."

He took a step toward her, hit a flow of moonlight washing through the window. Faded lipstick kisses decorated his hard body.

They needed to be erased.

But she didn't dare touch him. Instead, she opted for the barred-arm position again.

"Fiona." Soft, low, terrifying in the dark of midnight. "I think you're shyer with your clothes on than off."

"It's all those questions." *Sure, Fi. Sure.* "They're invasive."

He was right in front of her now, all strained power, temptation. What if she could just lean her head against his chest and close her eyes?

What would happen?

She tightened her arms.

"Don't get all worked up," he said, chuckling. "Lakota and I dropped by a perfumery today. Did you know they'll mix a scent that belongs just to you?"

"Sure."

"Hell, I had no idea."

"So you and Lakota were getting in some quality time?"

He lifted a rugged eyebrow.

"Strictly a business query," she said, putting him in his place with a grin. "I noticed a definite... change...in Lincoln today."

Suspicion drew his mouth into a line. "Yeah?"

Like she was going to blab Linc's love secrets to Mac, Lakota's keeper. "I think things will improve from here on out. He's not going to mess up any-more.''

Mac put down his beer, faced her straight on. ''Same with Lakota.''

He hooked his index fingers under her nightie straps, lifted, drew them away from her shoulders.

Fiona gulped. ''Well. Then we won't need to worry about those two clowns. Will we?''

''That's optimistic.''

With lethargic purpose, he positioned her straps just so, then let go. The material fluttered downward, caught by the tips of her breasts. The lace scratched against them, pinpricks of sensual delicacy.

''Mac…''

''You chickening out?'' He knuckled over one nipple, and it contracted.

''Never.''

''Game on, then.'' He bent, taking her earlobe into his mouth. Sucking on it, he caused her to clumsily abandon the beer, to abandon all pretenses.

Why not indulge herself a little longer?

He guided her backward, until she hit a stool with the backs of her thighs. At her sharp intake of breath, he lifted her, hefting her on top of it. Pushing up her gown until it gathered around her hips, he pressed on the inside of her thighs until the air throbbed over the naked center of her, leaving her open. Vulnerable.

She anchored herself, bracing the arches of her feet on the most convenient rungs, struggling for balance. He glided his lips to her throat, lightly plucking at her neck veins with his teeth and tongue, traveling down, over her chest, between her breasts.

A strangled mew wrenched from her throat.

She pushed against him, but he urged her farther against the stool, the wall. Through the gown, he licked a nipple, wetting the material, and making her suck in much-needed oxygen between her teeth.

Mac had the upper hand, and he knew it. The thought spurred her into action.

She squirmed away from his mouth, laughing. "What's *your* favorite spice?"

Stalemate.

His breathing rasped against her shoulder, and he backed away, snarling.

Pumped to go.

It looked as if he'd consume her whole if she gave in. His chin was lowered, his hands curved by his sides, his posture stiff, ready to prowl.

Oh, the power. The knowledge of having a man by the short hairs because he wanted her so much.

She almost hated herself for basking in the feeling.

Hated the feeling altogether.

But she couldn't help it. His frustration stoked something inside her. Something she lacked.

His steel-band shoulders rose with every violent breath. "Why the hell do I put myself through this?"

Fiona flexed her torso forward, watching a muscle tic in his jaw. "Because you're an addict?"

Even if he was aroused, she could feel him mentally pulling away. That wouldn't work. She was here to win.

With a slow, tortuous tug, she pulled up her gown, gathering it until she was open to him again.

Posting her foot against the side wall, she got comfortable, skimming her fingers over the inside of her thigh.

"See something you like?" she asked.

He thunked against the counter, watching.

Her fingers sought the folds of her sex. Even at this point, just with the banter, she was hot and sleek for him. Pressing a finger to one side of her clit, she applied pressure, getting off more from the rapt expression on his face than the actual act of touching herself so shamelessly.

She crooked the finger of her other hand at him. "What are you waiting for?"

His only response was to slide the cherry and jar down the counter, nearer. She knew exactly what he had in mind, and she pulsed with the anticipation of it.

He dipped two fingers into the jar, stood over her.

She pushed on her mons, the added weight making her restless. Dammit, she wanted it to be him, rubbing, building her up. *Him.*

Silently, with only the hum of the refrigerator to accompany him, Mac stroked the cool juice over her, fluid strums guiding her hips in time to his patient demands. The syrup felt sticky, heavy.

Then he took the cherry in his other fingers, an outlaw's grin on his lips. Holding it by the stem, he hovered it over her mouth. She went for it, but he jerked it away.

Who was in control now?

Her conscience skipped over itself, repeating the question.

He bent to his knees, placing one of her legs over his shoulder. The back of her knee stuck to his skin.

As he fastened his mouth to her inner thigh, he watched her, nibbling, playing his fingers over her pounding clit. Then, once inside of her, making her ready for bigger and better things.

She thrashed, rocked against his hand, threatening to upset the stool. He held her steady, chuckling.

"Come on," she said, hanging on for dear life.

"What's your favorite music?" asked his muffled voice.

"Mac."

He drew away. "Answer."

She winced. "Um. The Police."

"Ah. A connoisseur of the eighties." He returned to the task at hand. "Good girl."

When his tongue connected, laving away the syrup, Fiona cried out. He circled the most sensitive part of her, sucked until dizziness drew her down.

He took one of her lips between his, let go of it with an insouciant slurp. "Favorite flower."

"You've got to be kidding. Damn—" Was that a sob? "Just…"

He moved an inch backward.

"Wait. Flower." She couldn't think. What were those things called again? "Roses. That's it. Roses."

She could feel his shoulders lift in a shrug. So it'd been a clichéd answer. Big deal.

It was good enough, she supposed, because he was back where he belonged. This time thrusting his tongue inside her, warm, mobile, swirling. Then... something else.

She convulsed, jamming her chin against her shoulder. He'd put the cherry between her folds, was eating it, licking, nibbling, consuming.

Heat flushed over her, poising her on a shuddering breath. He held her hips as she whipped from side to side, agitated.

She cried out, banging her head against the wall, devoured by a flare of stillness, then a surge of crashing sensation. She grasped at it. Pulsating waves pounding from the inside out, tearing her apart, ripping every shred of emotion and turning it into a physical nerve.

She muffled a cry. Still, his mouth was on her, driving her toward a red wall. Closer, closer, farther, closer...

It shattered as she smashed into it, ramming forward, backward, again and again. Pinpoints of release tingled her skin, moistening it with beaded sweat.

She couldn't catch her breath, couldn't grasp onto anything. Lost, broken...

Oh. There.

Satiated.

She didn't want to open her eyes, didn't want to expose how much she wanted him. Yearned for him.

Breathe. Control.

Finally, she pulled herself together, then chanced a glance. Good thing she'd waited, because he'd been observing her, one hand still between her legs, the other covering her up with the nightgown. He had something in his mouth, and when he took it out, Fiona couldn't help a contented smile from arching over her lips.

He offered the cherry stem to her. It was tied into a knot, just like she used to do in college at the bars, impressing all the boys.

"Done," he said, cocky as ever. Then he went back to his beer, saluting her with the bottle, as if nothing had transpired from point A to point B.

The shakes started up again.

"Done?" she gasped, sliding off the stool. "I don't think so."

LATER THAT NIGHT, after he'd driven into her, spilling himself into a condom time and again, Sean had finally drifted off to sleep. A deep sleep, for the first time in…ever?

He rolled over the TV room carpet onto a blanket, where they'd ended up after a bout with her propped on the kitchen counter, a session in the bed and one in the hallway.

Groggy, he sought her out. Finding her. Drawing her against him because it felt so damned good.

Even though he hadn't bothered to open his eyes, her image was still imprinted on his mind. He didn't have to look to see her. Feeling her bare breasts against his chest was enough.

Content, he must have drifted off again because, when he did officially awaken, it was because the phone was ringing. Sunlight streamed through the windows as he woke up. Something feathered over his face.

He opened his eyes to find Fiona stroking his cheek, watching him.

As the phone screeched, he shifted. She jerked back, creating distance, especially in her dark eyes where he could've sworn something mysterious lingered.

Quick as summer lightning, she turned on the Cruz charm, hiding behind a sexy come-hither expression.

Bitter disappointment filtered his vision, making him glance away. What was his problem? He didn't want a woman gleaming onto him, choking him.

It was time to let her go, wasn't it?

The words "you lose" were busting his teeth, trying to get out. But he couldn't say them. Didn't want to, because if he opened his big mouth, the bet would end. Done. No more sizzling sex. No more pretending that neither of them gave a crap.

And that's what made being with Fiona so much easier.

"The office is calling, sleepyhead," she said. Raising her arms up, she gave him an agonizing view of her curvy torso, her full breasts.

So she thought she'd gotten away with it. Emotions. But what did he know? Maybe he was wrong, and she'd been waking him up for another go-around.

But what about her eyes? That look?

Sean braced himself for the terror, the urge to flee, but it didn't happen. Instead, he wanted to see the softness again.

Or was this just that after-glow bullshit he'd heard about?

The answering machine picked up the call as they both sat there. Fiona leaned back on her elbows, casual, careless. He rolled over to his stomach, burying his face in his arms.

Damn, he was sore. And it felt great.

"McIntyre," barked Louis Martin's voice. Luckily the boss man had the machine to guard him, or else Sean would have busted the guy against a wall.

"It's Saturday morning," said Fiona, all sing-songy. "Tell me he's not expecting you."

"Where are you?" Louis went silent, probably expecting Sean to pick up.

"I'm there most weekends," Sean said. "I guess he's starting to take me for granted."

Louis made a coughing noise, then hung up without saying anything more.

Both Sean and Fiona said, "Moron," at the same time.

Fiona zapped a finger in Sean's direction. "Jinx!"

"Got me." He rested his head on his forearms, appreciating her skin, every inch of it. Appreciating too much.

Fiona stood, hardly bothered by her undressed state. And no wonder. Though her hips and ass were what could be called, "Rubenesque," she didn't have an ounce of fat on her.

"Playtime's over, I suppose," she said.

"Fiona."

Just let it go. Let her go.

She waited expectantly.

Hell, what should he say now? "I've, ah, got to be out of town for a few days. Got to visit a client's celebrity restaurant in New York. Touch base with connections there."

Her expression didn't waver. "Have a fun time. See a Broadway play for me."

"Plays. You like plays."

She hesitated, then shrugged. "Love 'em."

He nodded, not knowing what else to say.

"Well, then." She walked away. "Take a bite out of the Big Apple."

"I'll see you when I get back?" Why'd that have to come out as a question?

Fiona ran a hand along his wall, silent. Then, "I don't know."

"What?" He stood.

Her answer was whiplash smart. "I'm not backing out, you understand. I've got a lot to do this week. I've got to put together an event for Joanie Heflin's Pilates clothes line, and I…"

She trailed off, and Sean cringed for her. She felt the glitch in their arrangement, too, but wasn't about to say anything. Fiona was too much of a competitor.

So why wasn't he reveling in victory right about now? Why wasn't he calling her bluff?

Maybe because she really doesn't feel a damned thing, said all his niggling doubts. The ones that had watched his father fade into nothing.

She'd left the room already, probably going to fetch her nightgown and coat in his room. She'd shed her silk after the kitchen, when they'd stumbled to their next athletic arena.

He followed her, planting his hands on his hips as he reclined against the bedroom wall. She was busy donning her gown, facing away from him.

His image mocked him in the closet mirror. Streaks of last night's sweat blurred the surface, and even now, he could see the hint of red lipstick burning into his skin.

"Wednesday," he said, watching himself say the words. "That's when I'll be in L.A. again."

She was in her coat now, ready to go. Smiling, completely ignoring the bigger issues. "Travel safely, Mac. Don't work too hard."

"Wait." He retrieved her lipstick from the corner, held it out to her. "You're forgetting something."

Morning sunlight glinted off the golden tube, winking, nudging.

Again, with the laugh. "It's another souvenir." She nodded toward his undies-and-bras corner, his shame. "Or maybe you'll need it in New York. You know, for those lonely nights when it's just you and... well... whoever."

Was she wondering if he'd pick up some woman to keep him entertained while he was gone?

He should, just for the hell of it. Just because she didn't own him.

As she pushed the lipstick back at him, she stood on tiptoe. Kissing his nose, she was as flirty as a feline playing with a ball of unspooling yarn.

"I mean it," she said, "have a good time."

And with that, she left, giving him her blessing to stray.

Sad thing was, he knew he wouldn't.

9

DAYS LATER, when Mac popped his head into her office, Fiona almost jumped out of the chair.

"Mac!"

Okay. She needed to tone it down, didn't she? After all, she hadn't missed him *that* much. She'd just watched a lot of TV and gotten caught up on a lot of work. Had gone to sleep at night staring at the ceiling, tracing her fingers over her skin and pretending he was there.

It was always like this at the beginning of an affair, wasn't it? You couldn't stop thinking of the person, couldn't stop the craving for them.

She'd get over it.

His grin drew her out of her chair. He came toward her at the same time. Oh, that scent, that body. Even covered by a classy, black suit, Mac made her feel like they were both unclothed, skin exposed and humming. Awareness vibrated between them, a reminder of the other night.

Lipstick. Cherries.

"You keep things on the straight and narrow while I was gone?" he asked, holding something in his hand.

The hand that had cupped her breasts, explored the center of her and worked her to a moaning peak.

Fiona tried to remain cool. "What're you hiding there?"

He almost seemed embarrassed as his fingers fanned open to reveal a tiny wooden apple with the words "New York" etched into it.

"Oh." She fought the softness, the sap of strength from her body. "You shouldn't have."

But she cradled the apple in her palm anyway. What was he doing buying her another present? If they'd included *his* possessiveness as part of the bet, she'd have whipped the pants right off him by now.

No. Ridiculous. He was merely trying to win that tropical vacation, courtesy of her checkbook. Trying to buy her with sweet gestures and false gifts.

She shouldn't forget it, either.

He shoved his hands into his pants pockets, didn't say anything. Not even an "I missed you, Fiona."

Well, then. There it was. "How'd business go?" she asked.

She wanted to touch him so badly.

"Great. Things are moving right along."

Things. It was no secret that Mac had some catching up to do within the company but, lately, you'd never know it. He was really on his way up, mainly due to Lakota and a couple new acquisitions, including a rising down-home indie actress and a hot Tiger-Beat favorite teen idol. An uncomfortable poke of competitiveness irked her, because she needed to be in the same position.

That's right. She'd caught Louis's telling glances as he walked by her office, checking her progress, keeping her working late into the night.

She ran a thumb over the apple and tucked it into her suit pocket, where she could touch it without him seeing her.

Well, then. Back to business. "So Linc and Lakota have a Soap Opera Channel special they're filming in the San Diego area this weekend. *'Getaways,'* it's called."

His sharp green eyes cut into her, but she had no idea what he was thinking. "I know. Did Linc invite you down there, too? Just as a thank-you?"

"He did."

"Funny, isn't it?" He sauntered over to a leather chair, claimed it by taking a seat, lengthening his legs. "How their fighting stopped on a dime. How they're getting along so well now."

"Coyness isn't your strong suit." She aimed her own sly glance at him. "You know well and good that they've started seeing each other again."

"Unfortunately, I've been Lakota's confidant." Though his tone was dry, there was a trace of warmth.

When he was done with Fiona, would he move onto the diva?

She chased away the sting of her runaway imagination, told herself she was concerned only for Linc's sake.

"They seem happy," she said. "I hope it stays that way."

"I know, Linc's got a way of getting too intense.

Unfortunately, Lakota gave me a rundown of their short but flammable history while I was flying to New York,'' Mac grunted. ''Compelling.''

She'd give half her coming paycheck to know what Lakota was telling Mac, but she wasn't about to ask him. Not directly, anyhow. ''I thought I'd join them at the bed-and-breakfast this weekend, just for some downtime. You?''

Mac changed position in his chair, edgy. Fiona smiled. So he had the same idea. They'd continue their bet in another location, adding some variety.

''Going down there's not a bad idea,'' he said.

Excitement zapped through her limbs. Could she wait until the weekend?

The last time she'd seen Mac, she'd drawn away from him. It'd been instinct, a reaction to having him catch her in a vulnerable moment. He'd been sleeping, and she'd been exploring the ridges of his face: his lined forehead, his strong nose and chin. His talented mouth.

God, what had her eyes told him when he'd woken up?

Hopefully nothing, because she'd recovered quickly. Plus, he hadn't called her on it.

She was safe for now. And she wouldn't get caught appreciating him again. It was dangerous. Not worth the heartache.

She returned to her chair behind the giant mahogany desk, a hand-me-down from the last occupant. But she'd adapted well, had made the desk her own after the first day of work.

"I guess I can drive down to San Diego after my event Friday night," she said, picking up a pen, prepared to look like Mac wasn't ruling her every thought. "Grace Paget, my actress-turned-pop star, is signing CDs and having a mini concert at Spinnaker's Records. Then I'm good to go for the weekend."

Mac casually extracted a Palm Pilot from his jacket, then accessed it. "I'll drive you from there."

He wanted to come to the signing? Wasn't that kind of...well...normal? Something a real boyfriend would do?

He must've seen the doubt written all over her. "Don't get excited. It's a matter of convenience."

"Sure." She relaxed. "And I'm *not* excited. Just—"

Her skin prickled into wary goose bumps. Louis Martin stood in her doorway, backed up by Fiona's assistant, Rosie. The young woman shoved her wire-rims back up her nose and made a here-we-go face.

"Louis," said Mac, obviously not glad to see their boss. "I'm back."

The diminutive man entered, uninvited, and sat in the other chair. Rosie stood, notepad at ready.

"I didn't see your report yet," he said to Mac.

Mac's bullet-path grin split the tension, and Fiona squirmed restlessly in her chair.

"I haven't written any report." Mac turned his attention back to Fiona, and she sent him a wink of solidarity.

Louis's face turned a mottled red. What a Napoleon complex this guy had. "I just checked Karen Carlisle's column online. Fiona, good job of getting Lakota Lang the exposure.''

Victory straightened her posture. "Thank you."

"But it's something the *Flamingo Beach* publicist could've done. You need more than Karen Carlisle." Louis leaned forward in his chair. "She's small potatoes, not to mention that the piece was boring. *B-O-R-I-N-G.*"

The air flushed out of her lungs, and she fought the urge to sink back in her chair. She'd been at Stellar for only one week. What did he expect?

Mac chuffed. "Fine job, Martie. Now can you spell ingrate?"

"McIntyre—"

"—Do you know how much effort we've put into Lakota Lang and Lincoln Castle lately? We fished the fat out of the fire with them." Mac stood, clearly irritated. "Fiona's damage control has been right on target."

He was protecting her. *Her.*

"Your soap stars run the risk of getting bland, and you know that's death for publicity," Louis said. "John Q public wants passion, spice."

Fiona couldn't stand it anymore. "Motorcycle crashes, near-death experiences, a stay in rehab? Is that what they want?"

Rosie was furiously taking notes in her corner. But at this, she glanced to Fiona, nodding emphatically. Right-on, sister.

Louis's smile was patronizing, to say the least. She'd seen that sort of gesture her whole life. From her brothers, when she'd first run out to the lawn to play with them. From the Little League fathers, who'd yelled at the coach to take out the girl and give their boys game time. From all her previous bosses, who didn't take her as seriously as they should have.

He continued. "All I'm saying, Fiona, McIntyre, is that you can do better. Capitalize on the conflict between Lang and Castle. It's what keeps the public hooked."

Mac came to stand beside Fiona's desk. "There's nothing to exploit right now, Martie. They're not fighting."

He wasn't mentioning they were back together. Fiona's respect for Mac shot up several degrees. Linc and Lakota didn't need the added pressure of having their personal lives spotlighted right now. Their cohosting gig this weekend would be enough, with them presenting the image of friendly co-stars.

She sent him a message of thanks with her eyes. Their gazes connected, snapped, sparking with contained fire.

Until they both looked away.

Louis got out of his chair, shook his head. "McIntyre, you used to be a force to be reckoned with. I don't know what the hell took the edge off, but it's gone."

The rest of the sentence hung from the ceiling, a looped rope.

And you could be gone, too.

Their boss left the office, but Rosie stayed, wide-eyed in the corner.

Fiona retained her professional demeanor, even though she wanted to comfort Mac, to tell him that he was great, that she...

That she *what*?

His mouth was set in a grim line. Fiona just now noticed that his dark blond hair needed a trim, and the realization tugged at her heart.

Rosie stepped out of her corner, her notebook in front of her chest. "Mr. McIntyre?"

"Yeah?" So composed, so beyond her.

"I..." She came closer. "Don't listen to him. We all know you're the best."

Oh, no. Hero worship. Ambitious Rosie was shining with it, almost coming off as a groupie or something.

Mac remained distant. "Thanks."

"And..." Rosie took a deep breath, laughed. "Okay, no more. You get it. I'm gonna go back to work." With one last, lingering, you're-such-a-god glance, she deserted them, flouncing her way into the hall.

Fiona didn't say anything at first. She was too bitter, and not only about Louis's criticism. "That must've lifted your ego."

"Jealous?"

Unbelievable. "Get your mind back in this game. The girl's choosing her allies, and she's picked you." Fiona pressed her lips together, then, unable to help herself, added, "And I'm not jealous, thank you very much."

Put that in your maraschino cherry jar and suck on it.

"I'll check you on that tonight," he said, walking away.

"Don't be so sure about yourself. You're not *my* Apollo."

"You'll come." He lingered by the door, laconic, confident. "Ten o'clock's good for me."

She shooed him away, pretended to be immersed in a random memo. The writing made no sense. Just a bunch of squiggles and numbers.

When she looked up, he was gone.

But that night, they would meet up again, and welcome each other home with teasing kisses and passionate scenarios. The bet continued, a game that was growing more serious by the day.

Yet Fiona knew that the last inning was approaching.

SPINNAKER'S RECORDS on Sunset Boulevard claimed to stock over 130,000 titles. On Friday night, it was a hip place to hang out, with young customers weighing in at the listening posts, the in-store radio station and coffee shop.

Lincoln was relieved to finally get out on the town with Lakota. Fiona had mentioned that the actress Grace Paget would be giving an acoustic rendering of her first album here tonight, so he and his...he didn't really know what to call Lakota...had agreed to attend.

In baseball caps and sunglasses.

Not that they were big stars, especially at their position on the lower rung of Hollywood nobility. But acting like they were couldn't do any harm.

They stood toward the back of the crowd, brushing against each other, the contact reminding him that they really were together again.

At least as friends.

He had to pinch himself every day. On the set, the status quo remained. Both professionals, both memorizing every line, both blocking out their scenes without even a meaningful glance, both nailing the acting with flair.

But at night... Linc reached out and squeezed Lakota's hand as Grace Paget launched into a love song. At night they "hung out," helping each other memorize up to thirty pages of dialogue per episode. Sometimes they'd vary the routine, going to dinner with their co-stars after they shot their footage.

They were "pals." And it was killing him.

When Grace Paget finished her set and retreated to the signing area, the sizable audience applauded. He scanned the room for Fiona, finding her in the background. She was assessing the crowd, taking up Grace's back.

Typical Fi. Always supportive.

Lakota slipped her arms around his waist, and Linc's arms curved up in surprise.

As natural as you please, she said, "I'm going to buy a copy of the CD. You?"

His hands slowly came down, rested on her upper arms. Wary.

Grace Paget wasn't his thing. Lakota liked pop, he liked jazz, but it was only a minor difference. "Not tonight. I think I'll browse the bins."

Leaning back, she tilted her head. Staring at him, she hooked her fingers in his belt so her nails grazed his belly.

He captured her wrist, halting her. "Kota?"

"Linc." She made puppy-dog eyes at him. "Are you ever going to touch me again? I mean, what's it been, days since we stopped acting like mortal enemies?"

"I wasn't sure what you wanted from me. I thought…"

"You thought what?" She pulled back, but he still held on. "That I wouldn't want you as much as the night we broke up? For Heaven's sake, I've been waiting for you to put the moves on me, boy."

He fingered a strand of red hair that had wiggled out from under her cap, as if hardly believing she was allowing him to touch her. "I didn't want to ruin what we have so far. This…I don't know. Peace. The appreciation of just being together."

"Ah." She laughed. "You are the biggest romantic dope I've ever met."

"I want to wait."

Bling. Where had *that* come from? But as soon as he said it, he knew it was true. He craved the perfect moment with Lakota, to make up for all the ugliness of their past.

She shot him a sidelong glance. "For how long?"

Until you say you love me, he thought.

They were interrupted by Sean McIntyre, who'd quietly come up behind Lakota's shoulder. Lincoln bristled, cupped a palm behind his girlfriend's neck.

Hey. She was his girlfriend again.

"McIntyre," he said, smiling because of the Lakota realization, not because of the interruption.

The other man gave a slight nod of acknowledgment.

Lakota grabbed Linc's possessive hand and enfolded it in her own again. "Sean! Guess what?" She didn't stop for his answer. "I've got an audition next week! I mean, I was going to tell you this weekend, give you all the details, but since you're here... You know."

She was beaming, and Linc couldn't help feeling happy, too. He knew how much Lakota wanted to get out of soaps. Maybe he would again, too. Someday.

Pride made him talk to McIntyre. "She's been asked to read for an action heroine pilot."

"We'll talk about it in Julian. You *are* coming this weekend, right?" asked Lakota. "You and Ms. Cruz can relax. Our soap PR person's taking care of everything."

"We'll be there," said McIntyre.

For a second, the spin doctor's mouth pulled itself out of its stolid line, and Linc's hold on Lakota loosened.

Was Fiona still sleeping with this guy? She was pretty secretive when it came to her affairs, but this one... The pieces weren't fitting where they usually did. McIntyre was a square peg in Fiona's usual pattern. For one, he'd stuck around a lot longer.

Applause filled the store as Grace Paget waved to the audience and sat down to sign her CD and movie posters. McIntyre glanced over his shoulder at the podium, but Linc wasn't sure he was taking in the singer.

That's when he saw Fiona send the guy a saucy grin.

Yup. Still screwing him.

Lakota detached herself from Linc, heading toward the signing line. "I'll meet you in the jazz section," she said, wiggling her fingers in farewell.

"Sure." He couldn't disconnect from her, couldn't pull back his heart, even though the distance was increasing.

"Glad to see you two are still cozy," said McIntyre.

"Don't worry. I'm not going to break your little girl in half."

McIntyre assessed Linc for a moment, probably testing him. Then, "No you won't."

Linc cleared his throat, facing the man head-on. They were the same height, same build, but there was a saw-toothed rustiness to the publicist's attitude that set them apart.

"Same goes for you," he said. "I mean about Fi. That you won't take advantage of her."

"Fiona's a big girl. She's really great at taking care of herself."

"And you, more than likely. I know everything about her. Just about grew up with her." Linc didn't know how much to say. Fi didn't get domestic with her lovers. Still, she might need a bit of protection, here. Linc just felt it.

"Listen." McIntyre put his hands in his pockets, nonchalantly withdrawing from Lincoln's impending attack. "All you have to know is that Fiona won't get hurt. Not by me, anyway."

"What does that mean?"

"She's a romantic death wish." McIntyre glanced away.

"I'm still not getting you." Linc stepped into the other man's field of vision, all the while knowing exactly what he was talking about.

McIntyre nodded, acknowledging Lincoln's persistence. His caring.

No doubt the PR rep was wondering why Lincoln and Fi had never gotten together themselves. And Linc wasn't about to explain.

"Fiona's made sure that our time together won't go beyond the physical," the spin doctor said. "Has she told you that much?"

Oh, jeez, Fi, not again. Not more games. When would she learn? "What is her grand plan this time?"

"Maybe she should tell you."

"Come on, man," Linc said, "I won't throw a punch at you or anything."

McIntyre held back an obvious laugh, making it painfully clear that he thought a street-smart pugilist could kick the ass of a weight-lifting pretty boy any day.

Lincoln didn't push the issue.

"You asked for it," said the other man. "We've got a bet going."

Why hadn't she told him? "A bet?"

"Fiona thinks she—representative of the female nation—can enjoy a straight-up affair without getting emotional, territorial or possessive.''

Linc's shoulders sank. She'd do anything to keep herself lonely, wouldn't she? In college, she'd been popular, always booked for the weekend, always a sparkle in her eye. Never in love. Then she'd met Ted.

He'd sent Fi into a tailspin that hadn't stopped whirring. Since then, she'd pulled out all the commitment-phobic stops in existence. Giving out fake names to the men she was with, inventing lives that weren't her own, breaking off emotional attachments before they had a chance to grow.

But a bet? He had to give it to her. It was an inspired creation.

"Normally," said Lincoln, "I'd ask you to step off. But Fi would kill me."

Before Linc's very eyes, McIntyre seemed to retreat into himself. Was he feeling guilty?

"She's had some real disappointments," added Linc, for good measure.

"Haven't we all." Without elaborating, McIntyre straightened, offered a hand. "See you down in San Diego?"

Had he made his point to the guy? Linc shook hands with him, his grip firm. "You hurt her and, dignity or no, I will go after your ass."

McIntyre grinned without humor. Then he stepped away, a shadow of a man heading toward the door, blending into the night.

Lincoln would have to keep tabs on Fi this weekend. Just in case.

10

EVERYTHING WAS doves-and-loves down at the Soap Channel *Getaways* shoot outside the small, but unique B&B.

Linc and Lakota, plus their employees, the crew and the soap publicist, were filming on Julian's main street. Located just outside San Diego, the western-flavored town featured homemade crafts boutiques and apple pie. Today had been filled with shots of Linc feeding Lakota caramel treats, with Lakota showing Linc around an abandoned mine, with them both lounging around the quirky B&B. As the humidity wreaked havoc with the stars' makeup, the crew did its best to portray Julian as a romantic escape, with cool-air promises of an autumn bluegrass music and apple festivals.

They would finish filming the special tomorrow, but it didn't affect Fiona since this was the soap PR's gig. She'd spent the day shopping alone, wondering why Mac had done his own thing and become so distant all of a sudden.

He'd been that way last night, too, after the Grace Paget concert and signing. During their two-hour drive to Julian, they hadn't talked much. In fact, she'd been relieved when he'd put on a CD to drown out their silence. Salsa songs, stirring her soul, convincing her that at least they had musical tastes in common.

Besides bedroom tastes.

Was he getting sick of her? Was the inevitable separation beginning? After all, he'd left her alone last night. Not that she'd invited him to her room, but...

She flopped onto her bed, with its horse-patterned comforter and cowboy furnishings. Each room had a different theme—hers was the Wild West. Apple tree branches, budding with the promise of a fall bounty, lingered just outside her window, and she had a whole cabinet full of western movies to keep her occupied.

So why did she feel out of sorts?

With a sigh of impatience, she dug through the VCR collection. *The Magnificent Seven. She Wore a Yellow Ribbon. The Good, the Bad, and the Ugly.*

This room was awful. And for more than just the obvious reasons. It reminded her too much of ranches, proposals, broken dreams.

A knock sounded on her door, and she dropped a movie cassette, heart slamming against her ribs.

She raised a hand to her hair. Still in fine shape. Sniffed her skin. Good old Mango Madness body splash. Not bad for a long day of wandering boutiques.

''Yes?'' she asked, airy as could be.

The last voice she expected was the one she heard. ''Fiona?''

Lakota?

Getting to her feet, Fiona smoothed down her beige linen sheath and opened the door.

The young star was alone, garbed in shorts and sandals, newly showered with her red hair slicked back from her heart-shaped face. No makeup. No threat of wrinkles.

Fresh as a daisy Fiona would like to yank from the dirt.

"Hi," Lakota said. Her tone was so sweet and guileless that shame slapped Fiona in the face.

She smiled, trying not to wish that Mac was the one standing at her door. "Come on in."

"Thanks." The girl entered, immediately spying the bed and sprinting toward it, hopping on top and bouncing. "Yee-haw! Check this out! You've got a down mattress."

Fiona merely watched, floored. Where had the sophisticate gone? Maybe this wasn't Lakota at all. Maybe one of those perky cowgirl dolls from the crafts store a couple buildings down had come to life, escaped, gravitated toward the washed-out wood and antique-laden hideout that was Fiona's room.

Hey, that scenario was far more likely.

She addressed Lakota, who was now inspecting a creaky lantern hanging near Fiona's bed.

"Mac told me on the drive down that you have a big audition coming up. Good work."

"Thanks. God, I love vintage." Lakota leaned on her elbows, stared up at a stagecoach-wheel light fixture. "Linc should put himself out there, too. He's much bigger than soaps."

"His agent's working on it." Fiona tilted her head, fascinated by this changeling.

"Cool." Lakota settled down, hanging her feet over the edge of the bed. "Sean told me he's in the Caveman Room. Isn't that someone's classic idea of irony? I've got the Paris Room, and Linc's got the Pirate one. Argh."

Fiona raised a brow, nodded and laughed at the same time. "Yes. Funny stuff." Then she gave her guest a quizzical glance. "Well. So you're going from room to room, taking the grand tour again."

Suddenly, the jaded actress appeared. She was hiding under Pippy Lakota's skin, but Fiona could detect her.

Lakota's smile was knowing. "Actually, I've been meaning to ask you something."

Big surprise. "Toss it out there."

"All right. Why didn't you and Linc ever get together? It's been nagging at me."

Direct. She could respect that in another woman.

When Linc and Lakota had dated, Fiona hadn't spent a lot of time with them. She'd been busy putting out fires at her old PR firm—to no avail, it turned out. But the few times they'd all gotten together, Fiona had known Lakota was curious.

Was Mac also? Would Lakota tell him about this conversation?

"Linc never explained?" Fiona asked.

"I never asked him. I don't want the answer sugar-coated, because that's what guys do about the women in their lives. They try to make their girlfriends feel better by lying about female friends."

"Fair enough." Girlfriend, huh? During her last

Lincoln heart-to-heart, he'd told her he was waiting for true love before "taking it to the next level" with Lakota again.

Linc. Her sensitive, poet-souled buddy. She'd watch out for him.

Fiona assumed a casual tone. "When we first met in college, Linc was acting in *Waiting for Godot,* and I was taking a stagecraft class, hoping to meet guys. I worked on his production."

Lakota wiggled, obviously wanting to get to the good stuff, the parts she didn't already know. Apparently, Linc had talked about Fiona to *some* extent.

"And...?" Lakota prodded.

"And he was a doll. All the girls wanted Linc, of course." Fiona hadn't made any female friends in stagecraft class; she'd hung out with the boys, as usual. So when the ladies had swarmed Linc, she'd beaten them to the punch. The winner. "I'd kidded around with him during rehearsals, had gone to his campus apartment with a few guys to drink beer and shoot the breeze. But at the closing night party, I got him alone, thinking there'd be a little action involved."

"Good luck," muttered Lakota.

Sexual frustration. Poor girl. "We did kiss, but that's where it ended. It was the most disgusting experience of my life. Not—" Fiona held up a finger as Lakota opened her mouth—"because of bad hygiene, you understand. Linc takes great care of himself."

"Yup."

"But it was like kissing something sexless for me."

Fiona shuddered. "I felt it in the pit of my stomach. God, it was very wrong."

"So it was like this invisible force field that kept you from him? Kind of like a magic spell? Because when *I* kiss him—"

Fiona cringed. She really didn't want to hear this. Girl-talk was not her forte. "I suppose you could say we're destined to be something other than...well... lovers. He felt the same way, because when we pulled back from each other, he had the most horrified expression on his face. I laughed out loud, the poor thing, but luckily he joined right in. We got along so well that we never stopped seeing each other. He's my special guy."

She imbued the last phrase with dead-aim significance.

Lakota got it, judging from the cool blue of her eyes. "What about Sean?"

Fiona's attempted laugh fell flat. "Here endeth the lesson. You got what you came for, didn't you?"

"Not entirely."

A tiny bleep of hope flashed across Fiona's radar. "Mac sent you to be a spy?"

"I look out for him, too."

Could this be any more juvenile? "Then tell him I don't pass notes during class."

Lakota frowned, then pouted out her lower lip in an adorable sign of Mac-attack sympathy. "Sean's a great catch, if you ask me."

Was Fiona actually talking about relationships? With another woman, no less? Part of her wanted to dig for more information. Part of her remembered that she had a bet going, and it didn't include giving a crap about Sean and his catch-a-bility.

With all the strength Fiona could muster, she walked to the door, opened it, sparkled a smile at Lakota. "Are you satisfied with how I answered your question?"

Lakota looked Fiona up and down, then slid off the bed, heading toward the hallway. "It explains a lot."

Fiona didn't take the bait. She didn't like to be psychoanalyzed, especially by a girl half a decade younger than she was.

She already knew she wasn't your garden-variety woman. And that was fine by her.

"Just do me a favor?" asked Lakota, stopping on the way to her room.

"The requests never stop."

"Go to dinner with Sean tonight. Do something to put him out of the funk he's in." Lakota dimpled. "The guy's sweet on you, so don't blow it."

Lakota left a shocked Fiona holding the door.

Holding the power to take the next step if she really wanted more.

"I HATE TO SAY IT," Lakota said, a half hour later, "but Fiona's got issues."

She skidded onto Linc's thick comforter, reveling in the way her bare legs and feet sank into the downy softness. Hopefully, by the time morning rolled around, the cover would be on the floor, the bedsheets tousled by some physical activity.

That is, if Linc was up to it.

He exited the bathroom, a towel cinched around his lean waist. Rivulets of water meandered down his firm chest, his rock abs. Lower, a hint of long beefcake pushed at the terry cloth, making Lakota press her thighs together, quelling the pump of warmth between them.

"She's always marched to her own beat." Unaware of Lakota's erotic state, Linc combed down his wet hair, standing in front of the closet to pick out clothing. "What do you want to eat? There's that café down the street."

Lakota rubbed her legs over each other, liking how it turned her on even more, her words thickening to syrup in her throat. "Let's dine in tonight."

He stopped fussing with his hair, then started again, ignoring the invitation. "They don't have room service."

"Linc. Can't you catch a clue? I want you to jump my bones."

The muscles in his back froze, then he tossed the comb onto a sea chest that doubled as a vanity table. They were in the Pirate Room, with its faux rope gilding, its cannon-and-doubloon decorations. Couldn't he get into the spirit and plunder her?

When he turned around, Lakota could see that his— how should she say it?—"cutlass of love" understood her needs. Now if only it could relay the message right on up to his oxygen-starved brain.

"I realize," he said, "that this is all very romantic. The shiver-me-timbers, the Errol Flynn movies…"

"...The damsel in distress." Lakota started unbuttoning her top. "Or no dress at all."

He covered his eyes with his hand, smiling, turning it into a joke. "I'm cutting myself off. No stimulus, no temptation."

Shoot. Hey, were guys as excited by audio cues as women were? Worth a try. She peered around the room for one of her historical novels. Preferably one with a high horny quotient.

D'oh. She'd left her books in her room. Shrugging, she finished taking off her top, leaving her in bra and shorts. Then she tossed the material away.

Phomp.

"Oh," she said. "That was the sound of a corset hitting the wooden planks."

"Kota..." He blindly waved a hand around, searching for something to talk about. "What were you saying about Fiona? You haven't asked about her since...well, a long time ago."

Lakota rolled her eyes. "I paid her a visit. She told me about your first kiss. Ugh."

"Exactly. Can I look now?"

She brightened, reaching for the clasps on her bra. "Sure."

"I can hear it in your voice. You're still half-naked on my bed. I'm going to have to send you out of here, if you're not good."

There, she'd gotten the bra off. Lace went flying through the air, joining her shirt on the floor.

He heard the plop. No doubt about it, because he

flinched when it hit. But he still wouldn't look. She almost had to admire his willpower.

"Do you think Fiona and Sean...?" she asked.

Linc peeked through his fingers. Then his hand dropped to his side.

Lakota preened, cool air from the conditioning unit, along with his suddenly hungry gaze, hardening the tips of her breasts. She loved how he looked at her—as if he'd been on a crash diet and she was a plate of hearty fare.

She scooted back, lying against the pillows, spreading her hair in back of her and allowing her arms to linger overhead. "How long do you think before Sean breaks Fiona's tender heart?"

Linc's throat worked, his Adam's apple bobbing as he struggled to swallow. "It'll be the other way around, believe me."

What was this? She was laid out before him like a feast, and he was just standing there? Was he waiting for something? More encouragement?

She crooked her finger at him, the exclamation mark on her body language. "It's your professional opinion that the two of them aren't going to last?"

Whomp. There it was. His penis stirring under the towel, tapping out Morse code to Lincoln Central.

He couldn't last much longer.

Lakota traced one hand between her breasts—small, but definitely adequate—over her flat stomach, unfastening a button, fingers loitering by her zipper. It buzzed as she opened it, allowing the gape of her shorts to reveal her striped bikini undies.

"I'm right here," she said, dragging out the words.

Clearly torn, Linc rammed a hand through his combed blond hair, ruining the previous effort at taming it. He puckered his mouth, blew out a breath.

At least she was getting to him. "What can I do, Linc? Should I go to Fiona's Cowboy Room and borrow a lasso? Or do you want to go down there yourself? Huh?"

He didn't say anything, just watched her.

"Is that it?" she asked, sitting up, her blood starting to simmer, melting all rational thought. "Maybe you'd like to sleep with your friend instead. Maybe she lied to me and you did put the wood to her all those years ago."

"Don't be unreasonable." He sat on the edge of the mattress, his back to her. "Don't let one more nonexistent 'other woman' ruin this."

Memories pummeled her. Cringing in her childhood bed, allowing "Lara's Theme" from *Dr. Zhivago* to carry her away, to block out the thumping and moaning, as those "boyfriends" had their way with Mom in the family room. Slamming the door to a run-down L.A. apartment and winding up that music box after yet another audition in which an old-goat producer had tried to stick his hand down her top while promising to further her career. Throwing that music box at Lincoln when he'd stayed out too late one night for no logical reason, chasing him away with accusations of "another woman" as the twisted metal scattered over the floor.

Why had she been so afraid of giving herself to him

fully? Was it because she knew he'd dump her as soon as he realized what a nobody she was?

On the bed, she shriveled into herself, drawing her knees to her naked chest, resting her chin on them. "I think I'm jealous of Fiona," she said softly.

"Why? There's nothing there." Linc turned around, placed a hand on her head, owning her.

That's right. This was the first step back into their rhythm. He'd claim her, body and soul. The thought made her claw for breath.

But right now, she leaned into his possessive touch, wanting it more than anything else. "She makes it seem so easy. Success. The whole *je ne sais quoi*. I want to be like her. To rule the world."

Linc laughed, petting her. "You're a human whirlwind yourself, you know."

The acknowledgment made her reach out for him, pulling him back to the pillows with her, just to see how much power she did have. "I suppose Sean will take that wind out of her mighty sails."

She could feel Linc's pulse beating through his skin, into her breast, into her own heart.

"You keep saying that," he said. "I'll bet he sinks first. And it'll be ugly, believe me. Fi takes no prisoners."

Lakota caressed his slanted cheekbone. He was so beautiful, with those deep blue eyes, the archer-bow lips. "You've got a bet, buddy. What does the winner get?"

He'd grown still, stiff. He was resisting her even now, with half his athletic body pressed into hers, his towel scratching her upper thighs, crinkling the piece of paper she had in her shorts pocket. "Winner gets a kiss."

Yeesh. "Is that it?"

He seemed crushed, didn't say anything for a moment. Then, "It's everything."

Her stomach pretzeled, going all goofy on her. His romantic streak was dangerous.

She shifted her hips, rubbing against his growing erection and nestling him right between her, where she could gain some amount of satisfaction. She was already slipping and sliding down there.

"I adore you," she whispered, her breath echoing warmth against his ear and back to her own mouth.

He laughed to himself. "I guess that's good enough. For now." Then he relaxed a bit, enveloping her in his arms, lowering his chest to hers.

Her nipples, sensitized to the point of delightful discomfort, combed along his chest. She loved that he had no hair there, was still wet from his shower and slick to the touch.

The sensation caused her to grind her hips upward, into his groin. At the same time, she licked the edges of his ear, huffing air against it. He'd always liked that.

And things hadn't changed. Linc growled, nipping at her jaw, her lips, sweeping her into a dizzying kiss.

As they sipped at each other, prolonging their first sensuous touch in months, Lakota dragged her fingers through his hair, lazily massaged his scalp and neck, moaned into his mouth.

The languid memory of their very first kiss washed

through her body: one night on a pier, the salted air tanging his skin, the sweetness of being chosen by the big man on campus, of being accepted.

The surge of that moment revitalized her, causing her to wrap her legs around him and work off his towel with her knees and hands. In response, he soared forward, one hand raking up her spine, the other pressing the back of her head, until their mouths smashed together, devouring.

She came up for air, panting, every pore of skin spinning in circles. "Protection time."

He groaned, resting his mouth against her neck, breathing roughly against her ear.

She worked her hand into her shorts pocket, came out with a form their managers made them sign before having sex with anyone. Standard biz practice. It proved consent, barred anyone from crying foul in the future.

As she leaned toward the night table and a pen, she said, "Tell me you brought the other coverage."

"Do you need it?"

He was asking if she'd slept with anyone since him.

She'd already signed the consent form, so she rested the paper on her chest while he applied the pen to it.

"It'd be safer to use a rubber," she said.

He placed a tender kiss above her top lip. "I haven't been without one since we were together, Kota."

"Please, Linc?"

She held his head to her temple, shut her eyes, nudged even closer. So close she could have crawled into him, blanketed in his warmth.

He made a sound of jagged disappointment, drew away from her, went to his half-unpacked suitcase and withdrew the condom. Unwrapped it.

In the meantime, Lakota pocketed the form, stripped off her shorts and undies, eager to feel him again. "Hurry."

She'd missed true affection, being with someone who cared. And Linc did.

He rested one knee on the bed, fitting the rubber over himself, then crawled the rest of the way to her, framing her face with his hands.

"I'd do anything for you. Dammit, I love you so much."

She hesitated. "Me, too."

Then, fevered, she led him into her, hardly needing any more foreplay.

With his erection prodding her, skidding into her so easily—just as if he'd never left—she believed that she loved him. Had never stopped.

She rocked against him, clinging to his moisture-beaded skin. As he pulsed into her, her muscles embraced him in a welcome-back clench, and he groaned out her name.

Their pace quickened. He braced a hand against the headboard and, faintly, she could hear it pound against the wall with every push of his hips.

The music box of her mind wound up, playing out of control, the tinkling strains of an innocent song racing to catch up with his hammering thrusts.

Mirrors—so many of them—flashed behind her closed eyelids. They blinded her, revolving, spinning until she was lost, confused, grasping for something to hold on to and coming up with nothing but air.

She squeezed her eyes shut, concentrating, moving with him, then...

Open. The room whirred before her, coalescing into crushed-velvet colors, crashing down on her with the reality of Linc, still buffeting her, still seeking.

She helped him, drove him on, sketched her fingers to his corded stomach, his belly button. Linc's most lethal erogenous zone.

She whirled her thumb inside of it, pressing, demanding.

"Kota..."

With one final strain, he came, quaking to a climax, crumbling to the bed. To her.

They breathed together, held each other for what seemed like hours. She took advantage of every moment, assuaging her neediness, erasing everything she thought was wrong with her by melding into him.

Finally, when their bodies settled into sticky-salty restfulness, Lakota entangled her limbs with his, creating complicated knots.

Never wanting to be untied.

11

SEAN DIDN'T KNOW what was what anymore.

Last night's conversation with Lincoln had really thrown him for a loop, so much that he hadn't known what to talk about with Fiona on their endless drive to Julian. Hadn't known what to say to her today, either, so he'd avoided her altogether.

She'd been disappointed in the past.

Why was he feeling badly about that? It had nothing to do with him or their present liaison. In fact, if he had any sense at all, he'd be doing the typical Sean McIntyre escape routine and hightailing it back up to L.A., minus one disturbing woman.

Still, he found himself outside her room that night, a bag of oranges in hand, knocking on her door.

While waiting, he leaned closer to the wood, hearing a few "whoops" and the rumble of wagon-wheel thunder over hard-packed ground.

The Cowboy Room, huh? Sure as hell beat a Caveman Room. The Pirate one had more appeal, quite frankly. Who's idea had it been to…?

The TV chopped to a pause, and he heard her moving around, coming toward the door.

When she opened it, the sight of her dressed in a

cute pair of pink shorts with a white top, her dark hair swept into a ponytail, crushed the oxygen from his lungs. A few loose tendrils framed her face, making her dark eyes liquid.

Something shifted in his chest, and he reached up to clutch at the strange tightness, catching himself, recovering.

"Speak of the devil," she said, frowning at the panicked expression that was probably on his face. "I was thinking of running by your room, seeing if you wanted... Are you okay?"

Sean brusquely pushed the bag at her, a decoy. "I bought too many things at the store. Thought you might want some."

Fiona's face lit up, and she took the bag, peeking into it. "Yes! Oranges. God love you. A snack is perfect because I had a big lunch with Linc's handler."

He'd seen Lakota's manager, Carmella Shears, at lunch today, himself, even though he'd been fantasizing about dining off Fiona instead.

They stood there for a moment, all the awkwardness of last night's drive, where she'd watched him with so many doubts in her gaze, coming back to the forefront.

"Well, then," he said, breaking the tension, "I'll leave you alone."

"Mac." She grasped his T-shirt, pulled him toward her. "We've still got a couple weeks left to whip me into an emotional mess."

Damned bet. How could she be so giddy and so aloof at the same time? It was almost as if she'd been encouraged in some way. God knew, last night, their humdrum drive hadn't scored any romantic points.

He remembered the way she'd looked at him that one morning, with her heart beating in her eyes as she stroked his face.

It was pretty close to the way she was watching him now.

Call the bet in, said one part of him.

No, said another. *Forget the bet. Run for your life. Give the both of you a way out. Save some pride. Do it before it's too late.*

"I've been thinking," he said, "that maybe this whole wager has gotten to be more than we bargained for."

Fiona's lips parted and, along with those pink-tinged, cuddly clothes, she seemed in need of comfort.

But she recovered, taking his arm, guiding him into her room, then shutting the door. "Maybe the hallway's not the place for this."

Right. Damned lapse in judgment. "Fiona, come on. Let's forget about it."

She shot him a flirty glance, the wounded girl gone. "What's going on, here?"

"Nothing, it's just taking a lot of energy, and Martie is being a real pisser lately. In case you haven't heard, my job's on the line."

A slight shrug. "All of us feel that way."

"But you're still the new guy. You'll get the benefit of the doubt. Me..." He shrugged. "Martie hasn't been shy about letting me know that you could be my replacement."

"Well, isn't that a great excuse for wimping out?" Fiona swayed away from him, set the orange bag on the bed, keeping the mattress between them. "I have to tell you, I've been tempted to back away from the bet, too. Because of work, of course," she stopped, cleared her throat, "but I'm not going to let Louis run my life."

She picked up the television remote control, fiddled with it as she plopped onto the bed, pillows fluffed at her back. On the screen, images of black-and-white mayhem had come to a halt: Dust hovering in the air from a wagon chase. Horses galloping, manes streaming in stiff glory. A cowboy's hat caught flying off his head.

Fiona stared at the frozen moment of action, then at him, grinning. "I'm set on winning this thing."

Deep down, he'd known she'd shove the offer right back in his face. That's what he liked about Fiona, though—her moxie.

He only wished she'd show some disappointment.

Again, something twisted behind his rib cage. Too low for his conscience. Too high for his libido.

What the hell...?

If you win the bet, you win Fiona, too.

The thought reverberated, bouncing around his head. He'd never thought of it that way.

Run, boy, run.

But it didn't happen.

"So." Fiona patted the bed with her hand. "Take a load off."

Bed. Mattress. Fiona.

What was he going to do? Walk away?

Or take a chance, sit on that bed, see where the next day would lead them?

Don't do it, said the little-boy-lost part of him. *Remember Dad?*

That odd fist of...something...thudding behind the protection of his breastplate told him to take a step forward. *Do it, do it, do it...*

"Kick off those boots," said Fiona, acting as if she'd always known he'd stay. "We don't want those Jolly Green Giants dirtying my comforter."

He pulled off a sarcastic shrug, took off the boots, smiling to himself. No one got to him like she did.

When he was settled, she shut off the movie and flipped through the cable channels. They peeled a couple of oranges while watching one of those ubiquitous "inside" entertainment shows.

"Our work rewarded," she said, pointing a slice toward the screen. She bit into it, and the scent of citrus sprayed the vicinity. "Umm. I sort of feel sorry for the general public."

He watched Fiona eat, enjoying the sight of her moist, sticky lips. "Why's that?"

She swallowed. "Because they have no idea how much of these programs are straight-out lies. It's all image fiddling. Sometimes, just being a part of it, I doubt *I'm* real."

"Sure you are. You're a puppet master. Nobody pulls your strings."

As she drew a knee closer to her, hugging it, Sean wondered if this was what real life felt like. Did normal couples relax in bed, talking about everyday, average things like mortgages and world news and the weather?

Talking about their days at the office?

He pretended they weren't who they were for a second. Him, in his white athletic socks, jeans and T-shirt. Her, in shorts and a ponytail.

Sean relaxed, rested his head on a pillow. Not bad.

Had his dad felt the same, once upon a time?

"Oh," she said, leaning closer, ponytail flopping against his shoulder, "there's Sissy Baker at the Midwest Celebration Awards."

Sissy was one of his new clients, a freckled country actress who'd gone through a painful divorce with Cubby Bryson, a Nashville singer.

"Look at her," said Fiona, sighing. "She brought her sister as a date. She's been doing that a lot lately. Cubby's a creep." She slid a knowing glance at him.

Professional pride took hold of Sean. He'd made certain that Sissy's sister, mother or brother escorted her to every major event, making her come off as the strong, pull-herself-up-by-the-boot-straps victim in the public's eye. It'd been working, too.

"I appreciate your vote of confidence." He ate a slice of orange, and it tasted better than any food he'd ever consumed.

"I wasn't kissing up to you, Mac. I meant it that first day when I said you were good."

He didn't dare glance at her. A woman who respected Sean McIntyre for something more than his skills in bed? Incredible. The realization branded him from the inside.

He was talking before he could stop himself. "You're a different breed, Fi. You know that?"

She drew away from him, her ever-present smile fooling him into thinking she was taking this lightly.

"That's what my daddy always told me," she said.

"What else did your daddy tell you?" His voice had lowered, too, enough so the scrape of an apple tree branch against the windowpane moaned through the room.

"He said I'd grow up to be anything I wanted to be." That filmy sheen of emotion misted her eyes. "Even now I make phone calls back to Iowa—yeah, Corncob, Iowa, if you can believe that—once a week. I talk to my brothers a lot, too. I was lucky to have them growing up. They tried to make up for my mom being gone. We all miss her, even today."

He could tell by the flight-ready angle of her body that they were treading on thin ice, here. Should they be talking about anything beyond superficial factoids? Bantery bonbons?

Sean rested his hands on his belly, showing her he wasn't going anywhere.

This was nuts, but he was doing it.

"I wish my mom never existed for my dad." There. He'd said it. Years and years of built-up bitterness and rage, and he'd been able to utter the sentence without screaming it.

Fiona snuggled onto her side, facing him, her hand

on his forearm. Comforting. Real. A warm, firm grip telling him she wasn't going anywhere, either.

At least not right now.

But would she eventually run off into the night, leaving him before he could leave her?

Lincoln's words pounded into his skull. *She's had disappointments in the past.*

Or would Sean stay true to form and end up being the biggest disappointment of them all?

"She just left one day," he said, referring to his mom. "I think only my dad knows why, but he never talked about it. Not to anyone. He's disappeared to the point where you don't know he's in the room anymore."

"Do you think that's what's going to happen to you?" Her fingers plucked gently at his skin.

"No." A remnant of bitterness snapped at him. He chased it away. "I don't know."

There.

Was she going to open up, even a little? He'd feel a lot better about his own loose talk if she did.

"You're not so alone," she said.

He turned his head to catch the empathy on the curve of her plump lips, the inviting velvet-swirl of her gaze. Hesitating, Sean leaned over, hearing the hitch in her breath, then brushed his mouth against hers.

Tenderly, he worshipped the angel-tipped corners of her lips, tasted the sharp sweetness of oranges. He reached one hand out to cup her jaw.

A shower of molten peace swept through him, chasing away the doubts, the fears, blanketing him in a moment of quiet breathlessness.

Unconditional acceptance.

It was their first real kiss. No urgency, no sense of trying to find something lost and unavailable. Just the slow, fluid connection of sipping her into him.

She responded, fingers locked around one of his wrists, her other palm pressed against his chest, welcoming him and pushing him away at the same time.

He wanted her to be pulling at him, beckoning him into a place where she owned the part of his soul that he'd forfeited a few minutes ago.

But when he released her lips, rested his forehead against hers, she reached for his belt buckle.

He intercepted her. "No."

Confusion engulfed her gaze. "I…"

He didn't understand, either. At least not when they weren't kissing or eating orange slices in front of the TV.

She was back to the bet, and he didn't know if he could follow her there.

She got off the bed and crossed her arms in front of her chest. "Maybe you should…"

"…Go?" He got to his elbows.

"Don't you think?" She was back, the old Fiona, chin tilted upward, playful smile in place. "I mean, I didn't tell you, but I've made arrangements to ride back to L.A. tonight with Casey, Linc's handler. We've got some work to do."

"I see."

No he didn't. Had he made a mistake, coming here, pretending they could be normal people?

Wait. Was she shaking?

That's it. Big error. The worst. He had no business toying with her—with himself—like this. Sean McIntyre had his life wired. Why change it now?

He got to his feet, put his boots back on and headed for the door. "So I'll see you in the office Monday."

"You're staying?"

"Why not?"

"Oh. Sure. See you then."

"See you." Sean said.

And he was out the door before he could look over his shoulder at her. Back in his Caveman Room before he could think straight.

He couldn't stop remembering her lips on his, gentle, just as soft with longing as his had been.

That night, he drove home, too. First thing he did was go straight to the corner of his bedroom. To the souvenirs.

Bras. Lacy underwear. *Playboy* centerfolds.

A tube of red lipstick.

He took a garbage bag, tossing away the mementos one by one.

He threw all of them out.

Except for Fiona's mark.

THE BETTER PART of a week had passed, and Fiona hadn't heard from Mac.

Actually, she'd made sure of it. The Pilates fashion show had required most of her attention since it was set to roll this coming weekend. She'd be traveling to New Mexico with her actress client to oversee the event, thus getting her out of the office.

In the meantime, she'd worked on the details from an airplane and a hotel room miles away. Far from L.A., thank God, because an actor who'd had his racy memoir banned by a Bible-belt library had insisted on asserting his First Amendment rights. He'd taken her to Kentucky, where he'd strutted in front of the press with Fiona's guidance. They'd gotten great play in the papers and news.

Success!

Yes, that's what she'd concentrate on. Work, work, work—

—Mac.

That kiss.

The one that had sucked her soul right out of her body.

The feel of it was inescapable.

Now, here she sat on Lakota's twilight-bathed sundeck, having accepted Linc's invitation to enjoy cocktails with them. Fiona ran the rim of her wineglass over her lips, tracing her mouth, cooling the reminder of Mac's tender lip lock.

Tender. Maybe she'd misread the entire night. Mac wasn't that vulnerable. He couldn't have fallen into the trap they'd set for each other.

Really, she thought as she sipped her Riesling, the best thing to do was avoid him.

Avoid her ever-increasing emotions for him.

"You've been quiet since you got here," Linc said.

"Jet lag," she said. "But don't you look smirky."

Linc's goofy grin led to a blush. Right, a blush, from America's soap king, a man women cried over when he made personal appearances. A man who was still surprised that he could cause such hysteria.

"Things are going well," he said.

"With the soap?"

"With everything."

There he went, getting all discreet on her. This happened when he got hot and heavy. Linc didn't actually kiss and tell, didn't go into locker-room graphic detail, but he did talk about his feelings with Fiona. For some reason, he was the only person in the world who thought her qualified to give advice on the subject.

Fiona patted him on the hand. He was holding a half-full water bottle in lieu of alcohol. "I'm happy to see you this way."

"And I hate what's happening to you."

She sat up in her chair. "What do you mean?"

"E-ah." That was his I-shouldn't-have-opened-my-big-mouth sound.

"Spit it out."

"It's…I'm used to seeing you a certain way. Restless would describe it best, I suppose. But right now… What are the words for it?"

"I defy description."

"You'd like to think so. It's McIntyre, I think."

Fiona crossed one leg over the other, bobbed her foot in its sling back heel. "I've got it under control."

"That's what gets to me." A coastal breeze spiked

up a tuft of Linc's blond hair. "Ted messed you up, and you've been dealing out revenge ever since."

Ouch. "Ted's history. But, you know, I should've paid a visit to him and Crissy while we were in Julian. His quaint ranch isn't too far away. I could've met their little baby, taken some horseback lessons from the one woman I considered a decent friend. And I was *so* prepared to ride the range, what, with having rested in my Cowboy Room at the B&B."

"I didn't think about that," he said. "Sorry, Fi."

"For what? For Fate's little ha-ha on me? I'm over it." Yes, she was.

Right?

He shot her a glance.

"I am." She drained the rest of her wine.

Lakota shuffled onto the sundeck. Arranging herself on Linc, she snuggled onto his lap and wrapped her arms around his shoulders.

Fiona wasn't sure what to say to her. Why invite guests when the girl had gotten bad news recently? Her audition for the prime-time pilot hadn't panned out. In fact, Linc had confided that the producers had pretty much played the great-another-soap-actress card and dismissed her before she'd gotten a chance to read any lines.

"Hey, Lakota," said Fiona, smiling at her. "How was work today?"

The younger woman sighed into Linc's neck. "Terrible. I didn't have any scenes with Linc."

He stroked his girlfriend's hair, keeping a firm hold on her with his other hand. "She ruled the world today, didn't you? One of her scenes should be used on her Emmy nomination reel.''

Lakota raised a brow. ''*Daytime* Emmys.''

Linc gathered her closer, if that was possible. ''Soaps aren't a bad thing.'' He gave an amiable chuckle. ''*I'm* a soap actor.''

''The best.''

Fiona wished she could cling to someone on bad days, too, but she couldn't imagine being able to. ''There'll be a million chances for you to get other shows. You're young.''

''Not for much longer.'' Lakota shrugged at the sad truth, then got out of her chair and returned inside the house.

''Is she okay?'' asked Fiona.

''Don't worry,'' he said, straightening in his chair. ''She'll be back in two seconds to tell us her plan for global domination. Quick rebounder.''

Fiona tapped her fingers on the chair. Sure enough, Lakota returned, a package in hand.

''I almost forgot,'' she said, handing it over to Fiona. She went back to Linc, nesting again.

Unable to witness the love-fest anymore, Fiona opened the box. Inside was a bottle of perfume. The design of it was chic, like the angles of a postmodern house. She took out the stopper and sniffed it.

''Mmm.'' The mysterious heaviness of jasmine with a tease of…what was it?…grapefruit?

She dabbed a drop on her wrist, replaced the stopper, rubbed skin on skin to spread the scent. ''Thank you,'' she said to the loving couple.

Lakota didn't change position. "It's from Sean."

Fiona froze. Suddenly, the smell overwhelmed her, enveloped her. Stifled her.

A phantom pressure tingled her lips, reminding her of his kiss.

Lakota added, "He went back to the perfumery and had this mixed especially for you."

"Well." Fiona didn't know what else to say. She was imprisoned in her chair, partly from embarrassment—because she just knew what Linc was thinking—partly from an instinctual urge to stay, to accept his gift as if he really did care for her.

Now the young actress was addressing Linc. "Told you Sean would win. You owe me a kiss."

Lincoln shook his head, adapted a couples-only tone of voice—just this side of baby talk. "He can't buy her off. Right, Fi?"

"What are you talking about?"

Linc laughed. "We've got a bet going."

An uninvited blush consumed her. She'd never told him about her wager with Mac. Why? In spite of her bravado, the bet didn't represent the proudest moment in her life, even though she'd convinced herself it was a dandy idea.

Now it was Lakota's turn to act amused. "We've noticed some fireworks between the two of you. And we're just wondering… How do I put this delicately, Linc?"

"There's no way."

Lakota focused on Fiona while resting against

Linc's wide chest. "Which master would beat the other one."

Master.

Player.

That's all she was, right? Mac, too. How could she have forgotten? People didn't change because of one kiss. Life didn't work that way. It was too uncompromising, yanking away promises just when you thought you had them in hand.

Though Linc had asked about Mac before, Fiona hadn't known about any bet her friend had made with Lakota. The unexpected wager took Linc one step away from her and one step closer to his girlfriend.

"God, Kota." Linc laughed uncomfortably. "Fi's got a heart, you know."

Act like you don't care, she commanded herself. *It's never bothered you before.*

But she couldn't.

"Maybe I do," she said, voice near a whisper.

"At any rate," said Lakota, caressing Linc's ribs, "my money's still on Sean. I mean, look at that perfume. That's manipulation if I've ever seen it."

Her underdog instincts roused themselves. Jasmine and grapefruit filled her nostrils, yet she fought the takeover of her senses.

So Mac thought he had her where he wanted her? Thought he could kiss her senseless, control her in the end?

Maybe that's all last weekend's kiss had been. Like the vintage nightgown, it was another "gift" to sway her to the losing side.

Ted's voice came to her over the phone again: *Crissy and I are in Vegas. We got married, Fiona.*

Long ago, she'd told herself that she wouldn't be owned again. Beaten down by disappointment.

When she got back from her business trip this weekend, maybe Mac should get a taste of manipulation, too.

She'd mix pleasure and control as carefully as the ingredients of an expensive perfume, creating a dose of superior game playing.

She'd convince herself that he had no hold on her.

12

THEY DIDN'T SEE each other for the next week and a half.

She was in Santa Fe, then San Francisco, then New York, tending to business.

He was in the office, manufacturing scandals and triumphs in L.A.

It wasn't until the eve of their bet's cutoff, a Saturday night, that they saw each other again. And, even then, it wasn't arranged.

Or so he thought.

Sean followed Lakota out of a rented limo that dropped them off in front of the foliage-encased Malibu mansion of a film producer. As the balmy air licked at his skin, the scent of jasmine reminded him of Fiona.

The perfume.

He'd received a breezy e-mail from her thanking him, and the message had left him isolated.

He wanted to see her again, kiss her. Hold her because, even now, she was running away.

The knowledge weighed heavily, the sort of pressure that had probably kept his father sitting by the window.

Lakota took his arm. "Boy, were we lucky to be invited. I just know tonight's going to change my life."

Loud rock music blasted from a hidden location beyond the mansion as he and Lakota walked to the door. The structure perched on a hilltop, overlooking the beach and acres of vineyard, with cottages dotting the climbing landscape.

"See," said Lakota, "by the time the sun comes up, I'm going to be on the wish list of every mover and shaker here." She gave her tight black dress one last sweep of the palm. "Do I look blockbuster?"

"Always." She'd brought Sean along to the party because she'd convinced him he could hook some more big fish clients here. Besides, he had connections, and Lakota could take advantage of that.

Linc had denied her pleas to come with them, and Sean couldn't blame the guy. These big Hollywood bashes were laced with drugs, alcohol, everything a person didn't need after a rehab stint. Linc had already arranged to meet his agent at El Cholo, the famous Mexican restaurant, anyway.

Not that it dampened Lakota's spirits. As she rang the doorbell, she seemed every inch the budding actress.

It was Sean's job to encourage this transformation into the big time, but it didn't stop his heart from breaking at the sight.

He didn't want to see this business devour Lakota.

"Thank goodness for Fiona," she said as a suited

man opened the door. "It might kill me, but I'll have to give her a big old hug of appreciation."

They walked in and were summarily escorted through the fabulous, black-and-white schemed premises.

"Fiona?" asked Sean. "What does she have to do with this?"

Wide-eyed, Lakota ran her hand along the furniture and the antique mirrors. "She's the one who told me to bring you. This house belongs to Johnny Calloway, the producer who's doing Terry Oatman's comeback movie."

Fiona really *had* been busy, obviously engineering Oatman's return to glory. Impressive.

The silent man led them out of the mansion, past the beach-inspired swimming pool, up a palm-shrouded path toward the music. Of course Johnny Calloway wouldn't tear up his lovely mansion. This was the party house. Sean noticed several other cottages peeking through the greenery.

And then they were inside, a Rolling Stones tune crashing out of a state-of-the-art surround sound system. There were men in suits smoking cigars and other questionable objects, women—starlets and probably hookers—in skimpy dresses giggling and hanging all over the males.

Lakota beamed, and Sean hoped she wasn't feeling at home. He didn't normally attend these things, but when his favorite client—he might as well admit it— had asked, he'd given in.

They wouldn't stay long anyway.

But he did recognize people he'd worked with in the past: powerful corporation owners, directors, celebrities. Wouldn't hurt to network and introduce Lakota to them.

He escorted her around the room for about an hour, all the while wondering if Fiona would show, finding it hard to keep his mind on business.

When he did see her, the room became a much more interesting place.

Decked out in a red dress, its sheer panels floating behind her like the fire of a flamenco dance, Fiona wore her hair down. It fell past her shoulders, a shimmer of waterfall softness. As always, her lips were painted with red.

His red.

Lakota was engaged in an intense conversation with an independent moviemaker, one of those cutting-edge kids who'd applied for about twenty credit cards to finance his first movie.

Lakota saw where his eyes were glued and nudged him. "Go get her," she said over the music.

His first instinct was to act like Fiona didn't matter, but he was beyond that now. Beyond pretending.

He winked at Lakota, making a mental note to keep an eye on her, even though she'd taken command of every introduction he'd initiated. Then, heart in his throat, Sean inserted himself in the circle of men Fiona had gathered just by entering the room.

Even though she had a smile for every guy there, she lingered on him, lowering her chin, watching him with more seductive promise.

"Mac? You know everyone here?"

He didn't give a shit. Instead of answering, he jerked his chin to a deserted corner, hoping she'd follow.

Fiona took her time doing it, too, finally extricating herself from the gossip and accompanying Sean to his chosen location.

"You arranged this," he said, grabbing two glasses of champagne as a waiter passed.

She accepted one. "Thought you could use some help in the office. In Julian, you sounded rather concerned about your place on the nine-to-five totem pole."

Is that all she'd gotten out of their stay in Julian? His concern about work?

What about that kiss?

"Thanks for the professional courtesy," he said, stepping closer, catching the scent of jasmine mingling with the summer humidity. "You're wearing the perfume."

"Why shouldn't I?"

"I don't know. After that memo you sent me..."

"Oh." She laughed, dark eyes gleaming. "I wasn't in the office to thank you."

"So that's why it came off the way it did. Like you have no idea what this has turned into."

Fiona innocently considered him. "Isn't that how it is with us? No tangled emotions to make sex messy?"

The reminder sat like lead in his belly. "You know better by now."

"So, the gift wasn't just another chess move in our

competition?'' Fiona tweaked his lapel, still teasing him. ''You've got no ulterior motives?''

He swallowed, reached out to touch her face. ''None.''

Her jauntiness disappeared, and she pulled back, lips parted slightly. ''Because I feel somewhat claimed.''

Rage and panic crashed together in his chest, exploding. His hand dropped to his side. ''Stop this, Fi. Stop pretending you haven't felt anything.''

''I told you. I'm not that type of girl.''

Was there a note of sadness in her tone?

She glanced toward the party, swishing the champagne around in her glass, smiling at the crowd. ''I never will be that kind of girl.''

A vein in her throat fluttered, and he knew she was lying.

''Tell me you don't want me,'' he said.

''Sure, I want you. That's been very clear from day one.'' She sipped, paused. ''If you're looking for someone to share in the fantasy you've developed about that SUV you said you'd never want, search out of town.''

''Somewhere like Corncob, Iowa?''

That got her. ''I'll never be her again.''

''Why?''

She hefted out a breath, seemingly exasperated. ''Sex is all I do. Remember? I have one full day to go until I win our bet, and I can prove I'm not possessive. Or territorial.''

"Your eyes have told me something else. Ever since that first night."

"Can you be sure?"

Silence filled his lungs. No, he couldn't.

Fiona shook her head, giving him a pitying look. Then she grabbed his hand, tugging him away, out of the party. He glanced toward Lakota, who was touching her throat and laughing with yet another guy. Conrad Dohenny, the box-office hunk of the moment.

She'd do fine.

He followed Fiona as she took him uphill, to another cottage. One with dim lights shining in the window.

"What do you have planned?" he asked, suddenly wary.

"You say that as if you're ready to give up the bet."

Damned wager. He was sorry they'd ever started it.

"Fiona." As she unlocked the door, he held her back, trying to draw her into his arms, to stop this before she ruined every idiot hope he'd discovered within himself.

"We don't need to do this," he said, searching her face for any sign of vulnerability.

But there wasn't much light around, and the darkness allowed her to hide.

"Wait here." She slipped inside, came out a moment later.

Silk flitted over his hand, and he retracted it.

His pulse started kicking.

Fiona placed her finger on his lips, quieting any

response. Then she slid the blindfold over his eyes, taking away the benefit of his sight.

He could only smell her. Hear her.

Touch her.

"Come on," she said, the pull of her voice luring him.

Right into the cottage.

WHAT SHE WAS DOING would cost dearly. But he was getting to her. Taking her over.

Stop pretending you haven't felt anything, he'd said.

Oh, but she had, and it scared her to the point of desperation. She couldn't deal with feelings, with being torn apart by betrayal again.

When Ted had dumped her, she'd told herself, told everyone, that it was no big deal. But once, three months after he and Crissy had gotten married, she'd seen them at a restaurant, and her appetite had disappeared for days.

She'd literally felt broken, her limbs heavy and ready to fall off. Felt like her ribs were cracking under the weight of her mortification.

What was so wrong with her that Ted had married someone else?

And why had he fallen in love with Crissy, who'd somehow wormed her way into Fiona's good graces for a short time?

See, that's why Fiona didn't make girlfriends. Even with females, it all boiled down to a battle—who would win, who would lose.

Most relationships were like that, unless you could

find someone exceptional like Linc, who was so non-threatening and sweet it didn't factor into the equation.

But Mac posed a different problem. Theirs was a contest of wills. Of who could contain the heat and come out on top.

So he'd called her on a tender moment. That didn't mean she wanted him body *and* soul. Did it?

She guided Mac into the cottage, his blindfold allowing her to soften, to stop hiding. As she watched the candlelight swallow him, she melted, losing her proper shape.

His tall body cast a shadow over her, and the trembling started again, deep in her gut, stealing her sense of self.

She let go of him and closed the door, led him to sit in a wide velvet chair. Then she adjusted the blindfold, making certain it was secure. Warped silhouettes danced on the walls from the flames, illuminating the matching ottoman, the canopied bed.

The woman she'd paid to prove her point to Mac.

She was wearing a dress like Fiona's, a garment with much more material than her usual job required. Fiona had met her in a strip bar when one of her "dates" had taken her there, intending to turn her on, she supposed. Oddly enough, she and Brigette—the woman's stage name—had hit it off, had experienced a grand old time with Fiona buying her date lap dance after lap dance from her new acquaintance.

Over time, Fiona had brought more men to the bar, fascinated by how they could lose all strength at the sight of a topless woman.

Feeling sorry for them, too.

So when she found out Terry Oatman's producer was throwing a party, Fiona had invited Brigette, knowing that these crazy get-togethers included all kinds.

Brigette was here to make sure Mac would learn, once and for all, that Fiona wasn't getting emotionally involved.

It needed to be done.

Fiona gestured Brigette forward. The blonde knew to keep her silence. She was wearing Fiona's perfume, as well, just to prove the point.

"You sit right there, Mac," Fiona said, her tone as lazy as a candle's dance. She stroked his temple, allowing herself the freedom of feeling, just this once, while he was blinded. Her head tilted, and she bathed him with a gaze that took in his rumpled hair, strong chin, arms that had held her that night on a bed of pure kisses.

"Is this what you really want?" he asked.

The question tore at her conscience, shredded all the lessons she'd learned up until this moment.

No feeling. No pain.

She moved forward, blocking out the slight injury of his words. "Evidently," she said, scratching her fingertips lightly against his emerging arousal, "this is what you want. And that's what's important."

Before he could answer, she placed her hand over his mouth, her middle finger sinking between his lips, lost in a wet kiss.

Why did he have to be so...so Mac? Regretfully,

she took back her hand, nabbed the velvet ties sitting on a nearby table.

"Remember," she said, "it's just sex." With care, she trussed up his hands, running her fingers over his knuckles once she'd secured him.

"I want you to tell me that afterward, Fi." He smiled, almost knocking Fiona over with the power of it. One glance at Brigette told her that Fiona wasn't the only victim. The woman fanned herself like Scarlett O'Hara on a sweltering southern day, then rolled her eyes.

"You know the part where I'm supposed to look in your eyes and find nothing?" He let out a low, gravelly laugh. "You'll see."

But he wouldn't. Not with the blindfold.

Fiona moved away, beckoning Brigette toward him, going to the stereo in order to turn on some lazy music that would drown out the throb of the bigger party downhill.

"Regrets," by the Eurythmics. The tune slithered into the speakers, the pulsating synthesizers contrasting with the chugging beat and the buttery smoothness of Annie Lennox's vocals.

Quietly, so she wouldn't give away her location across the small room, Fiona spread her hands over her face, blew out the trembling breath she'd been holding.

Brigette gave her a shall-I-go-for-it? glance, and Fiona eked out a nod, muscles fighting the approval.

The stripper started by gyrating to the electronic drums, getting into the groove of her job. Then, she bent to her knees, slid her hands over Mac's lower thighs.

Oh, no. Fiona's eyes automatically shut, but she forced them open again. This wasn't supposed to be bothering her.

Mac had unclasped his hands, spreading them out in front of his chest. His nostrils flared, and Fiona knew he was relying on his remaining senses to connect with her.

Did Brigette's skin react with the perfume the way Fiona's did? Did he want the dancer as much as he said he wanted Fiona?

As the woman sketched her chest up his shins, parting his legs, Mac leaned back his head.

His reaction knifed at her, screwing, bladelike, into her belly.

But his jaw was shut tightly, his fingers still spread as if warding off the sexual advance. Her pulse gave a tiny jump, a spark escaping from a fire.

"I want to see you," he ground out.

Brigette backed off for a minute, seeking Fiona's tacit advice. It was a moment of sweet relief.

Fiona took a step forward without thinking, stopped herself. Was this Mac's way of manipulating the bet again? If she showed weakness here, revealing herself, she'd lose. Everything.

She couldn't give in. Not after she'd promised to never hurt again. Not after the way she'd suffered before.

Fighting the urge to give up, Fiona motioned for Brigette to continue.

The dancer paused, glancing at Fiona with concern. She was losing it, wasn't she?

Go, Fiona motioned, and with one last gaze, Brigette turned around and coasted over Mac's lap, rubbing her workout-tight butt over his thighs, pressing into him, back, nearer his groin.

Fiona paced toward them, fidgeting with her hands. Brigette winked at her; she'd been instructed on how far to go. They weren't friends, but the woman was a professional, knowing her tip would be higher if she obeyed instructions.

As Brigette gyrated, Mac strained, cursed, rested his forehead and hands against the dancer's spine. And Fiona knew the exact moment he realized the body wasn't hers.

He straightened, and his mouth went as tight as barbed wire.

"Go, Fiona," he said, strangled.

His anger almost brought her to her knees, slumped with relief. Thank God the dance was over.

He didn't want the other woman, did he?

So when was the buzz of power and victory going to screech through her? Shouldn't it have happened by now?

It only took her three strides to cross the room. Gathering herself, Fiona daintily helped Brigette off Mac's lap. The other woman stood to the side, waiting.

"Territorial?" Fiona asked with a hint of trembling flirtatiousness, untying his wrists.

She coaxed the blindfold from his gaze, tried to smile at him. "Possessive?"

His pupils contracted, adjusting to the dim light, closing in on themselves until she thought he'd leave her altogether.

He sat rigidly, almost threatening in his growing rage. "What's this about?"

"Isn't it obvious?"

Fiona stood next to Brigette. The blonde rested a hand on Fiona's shoulder, then ran the inside of her calf over the outside of Mac's leg.

She'd wanted to see how he'd react to the invitation, no matter how remote the possibility of it happening.

Red began to creep up Mac's throat, his face. The color marked him.

Fiona lifted an eyebrow, fighting for composure. *He didn't want the other woman.*

Adrenaline, cold and insistent, built in her. *Run.*

Mac shook his head, glared at the carpet. Then, to Brigette, he said, "Will you excuse us?"

"You sure?" she asked, doing her job very thoroughly.

With subtle precision, Fiona lightly pushed Brigette toward the door.

"All right, all right," the woman said. "Tough crowd."

Fiona wouldn't look at him. Wouldn't sink into the disappointment in his eyes.

She was *this* close to winning. Wasn't that what she wanted?

Fiona went to where her purse lay in the corner, and she paid Brigette, who efficiently left them alone as Fiona turned off the stereo.

Keeping her back to Mac, she glued herself together. Returning to her old flippant self.

When she turned around, Mac was on his feet. If she'd expected that gunslinger stance, she was in for a rude awakening. In lieu of an intimidating glare, he wore disappointment.

It was worse than taking a bullet.

"You're a piece of work," he said, voice dry. "You really aren't going to change."

For years she'd trained herself to survive. To avoid caring. And, see, she'd let him down. But better to have the inevitable goodbye now rather than later, when it would hurt even more.

"I never promised more than a good time," she said. "I don't turn into a quivering puddle of emotion just because of a bottle of perfume."

"Or a kiss," he said.

The music from the big party knocked around the room, and a sob worked its way through her chest, decimating everything in its path. Still, Fiona held on, controlling the damage. After all, that's what someone in her line of work did best.

Finally, he spoke, his words as heavy as rocks being pushed up a mountain.

"I'm sorry for you, Fi. I'm sorry for the both of us."

He watched her, the area around his eyes bruised, even though the rest of his tough skin didn't show it.

Then he walked out the door. She started to go after him, but couldn't manage more than a step.

"Sean?" she said, voice caught in her throat.

But he was gone.

Hadn't she known all along that, in the end, he'd walk away from her?

Because she always managed to make sure of it.

13

WHEN LINCOLN PHONED Lakota, telling her he had great news, he didn't expect to find her celebrating with the summer's biggest action star at The Cool Cat Lounge.

He didn't expect to find Conrad Dohenny's arm around her while they leaned against the glowing blue bar in the midnight-dark room. Didn't expect the flare of crimson jealousy that shrouded his gaze as he watched them: Conrad with his grunge-glamour, shoulder-length brown hair, his lanky frame pressing nearer and nearer to Lincoln's girlfriend.

Knocked for a loop, he could only stand among the throng of pretty people and watch, stunned.

He wanted to wring the guy's neck, no matter where Dohenny ranked on the Young Hollywood power lists.

Linc took out his cell phone, dialed Lakota's number. Obviously a little tipsy, she glanced around, tossed up her hands in goofy realization, then accessed the call.

"H'lo," she yelled over the lounge noise.

A cigarette girl swayed by him in time to the Rat Pack-era music, winking. Even though she was your basic L.A. beauty, her gesture didn't affect Linc. "Kota, what're you up to?"

Laughter. Linc could see Dohenny trying to get the phone away from her.

His confidence slipped. He'd trusted her, not only day to day when they did their scenes together, but with his heart. Had he been wrong to do that?

She used her arm to keep Dohenny at a distance, and Linc's spirits lifted.

"I told ya," she said, slurring slightly, "I lef' the party with some new friends and came to The Cool Cat. Where're you? 'S noisy."

She glanced around, as if he might be there, but Linc didn't bother to hide. No matter. She didn't spot him since she was now focused on Dohenny playing with her hair.

Don't fly off the handle, he thought, all his rehab training rushing back to calm him. *Center yourself.*

"I'm coming to take you home," he said, then flipped the phone closed with more force than was necessary.

She stared at her cell phone for a moment, then tucked it away into the little black purse that matched her little black dress.

How could you have a relationship with someone if you had to keep an eye on them all the time? She said she loved him, and he believed her. But what should he be thinking now?

Out of the corner of his gaze, he saw a guy wearing a rumpled button-down shirt, jeans and an assassin's focused intensity inching toward the bar.

Linc bristled. Smelled like paparazzi. Worse than the stench of booze, a bane which made him sick enough to dull the craving.

He was headed toward Dohenny, a favorite tabloid magnet because of his "bad boy" image. And now the movie star was whispering in Lakota's ear. She was listening, leaning against him, the worse for wear after a drink or two. Linc knew how Lakota got when she'd had too much alcohol.

Careless. Just as he used to get.

When Dohenny bent to bite at Lakota's neck, Linc shook his head, managed his temper. Okay. That was it. He hadn't wanted to embarrass his girlfriend, hadn't wanted her to know he'd been spying like the world's biggest loser from across the room. But what choice did he have now?

He made his way toward them, but not before Lakota pushed at Dohenny. He didn't take the hint, cupping her head in his hands, darting his tongue in her mouth.

Jeez. Why'd he have to go and do that?

A flash went off and, at first, Linc thought it was his impulsive fist whipping out to smack Dohenny. But that wasn't it. Both Dohenny and Lakota were glancing toward the photographer and the mini-camera he was holding.

There was a shouted curse, a general stir among the hip, young crowd. Varying levels of celebrities shifted, avoiding the scandal or running to it, as one of the men in the star's entourage grabbed the assailant by the collar.

"How the hell did you get in here?"

The photographer swatted at the bodyguard. "You have no right to touch me like this!"

The beefy men took the skirmish outside, securing the camera in the process. And that's when Linc stepped in.

Dohenny had resumed his pawing of Lakota and, as she swatted his busy hands away, she glanced up. Saw him.

"Lincoln!" She swayed, smiled brightly, genuinely excited to see him. "Conrad, this is my boyfriend I was talkin' about."

The star seemed unconcerned, his long-lashed blue eyes unfocused. "Oh."

"Linc, Conrad's gonna get me a part in his next movie. Sweet, huh?"

Usually, Linc didn't make a big deal out of his height or build, but he used both to full advantage as he hovered over the smaller star. "I'm sure he will, Kota."

Dohenny looked away from Linc. The jerk had been lying to her. He'd probably been expecting to notch another mark in his bedpost tonight.

Without blowing his top, Linc gently took Lakota's elbow. "Let's go now."

He led her away, but Lakota hesitated. "This is a professional," she mangled the word slightly, "opportunity!"

"He's not serious." Linc persuaded her to follow him again, getting as far as the lit candles fluttering inside the blue glass cups near the lounge's entrance.

Security cameras and bouncers lingered nearby, as well, keeping the club exclusive. Heck, Linc wouldn't have even gotten in if he didn't know the bouncer.

She skidded to a stop, glassed-in flames playing with the red highlights in her hair. "I was working my connections, ya know."

"You can make it without sleeping around."

Her speech slowed, sobered. "How do you know?" Those pale eyes grew huge, the sheen of tears covering them.

"Because I've still got a little faith in you." He held her face in his hands, unable to stop a smile from stretching across his mouth. "Even a schlep like me can make it on something resembling talent."

She glanced sidelong at him, grabbing onto his arms for balance.

He couldn't hold his news inside anymore. "My agent told me that Roger Reiking's daughter is a big fan of mine. She showed him *Flamingo Beach,* and he requested that I audition for a role in a romantic comedy he's putting together. A featured role."

Lakota just stared at him, as if assimilating the words. Wasn't she happy about this?

"He's probably only making his daughter happy," he said, miffed by her reaction. "What's wrong? It's *the* Roger Reiking. You know, Oscar-winning director?"

She blinked. "I'm happy for you." Then she laughed, combed her fingers through her already disheveled hair, hugged him. "It's just so surprising, is all. I'm ecstatic for you."

He remembered her failed audition for the TV show, remembered how much she wanted stardom and he just wanted to be lucky enough to earn a living acting—in any capacity. "I'm sorry."

"Don't you apologize." She disengaged from him, wiped away a tear, made a dorky sad/happy face. "Look, I'm so joyful, I'm crying for you."

God. He could feel it already—the tension, the inferiority of her staying in the soaps while he took bigger chances.

"I won't leave you. I'm probably not even going to get it, so..."

"You won't leave me behind?" For a second, hope brightened her smile, but then it crumbled. "You're meant for big things. I'm not." She started tearing up in earnest. "I'm gonna hold you back."

"You won't. Aw, come on, stop crying." He smoothed her hair.

"The thing is," she said, backing away from him, "I'm envious of you. Truly. I don't know if I can stand it."

Would she have been able to say that to him all those months ago? Or, instead, would one of them have sabotaged the relationship, avoiding the real issue?

Competition.

"We'll work this out," said Linc, reaching out a hand for her to take it.

She looked longingly at his outstretched fingers. Linc felt his throat close up.

By this time, Conrad Dohenny had gotten tired of

the bar and weaseled up behind Lakota. He set his hands on her shoulders, and Linc's chin lifted in response.

"There you are," said the box-office champ.

Lakota didn't move, just watched Linc as if he was going to drop her high and dry.

"Man," he said to Conrad, smiling amicably, "you really don't get the hint."

"Who are you anyway?" asked the movie star, puffing his chest. "You're nothing. So shut the hell up."

Dohenny pulled at Lakota's dress, stretching it.

"Hey," she said, drunken slur returning with a vengeance. "This is a DKNY original. Do ya mind?"

"Do you?" The star raised his eyebrows, and the candles spotlighted just how bloodshot his gaze was.

Booze. Jeez. "Listen," said Linc, "she told you to leave her alone."

Conrad stepped around Lakota, and she stumbled backward against a wall. A candle chinked against the wall, the flame wavering.

The star's entourage had gathered in back of him, as if Linc was going to start something and they'd end it.

"Hey." Linc held up his hands, palms out. "Let's just call it a night."

The bantam rooster pushed Linc, barely nudging him.

Great. Why did everyone assume that, just because he had muscles, he was eager to fight?

Linc held his ground. "Now, that's not necessary."

Conrad turned to his cronies, laughing. Then, without warning, he lowered his head and rammed into Linc's chest, throwing the bigger man into the wall.

Glass crashed, and Lakota screamed.

It didn't take long for Linc to make Conrad back off. All he had to do was get him in an armlock, then push him toward the entourage, but they swelled over Linc, jamming him against the wall again.

He didn't even see the fire as it slurped along the curtain.

Minutes later, the bouncers broke up the fight and helped Linc put out the flames by spraying the area with extinguishers, but not before the entryway had been damaged. And certainly not before the skirmish had been caught on the security camera.

As Linc and Lakota stood by, Dohenny's handlers calmed the star down. Too bad the soap actors hadn't traveled with their own personal assistants or handlers tonight. They could've used the company, also.

But Linc did the next best thing. He got out his cell phone and dialed the number of the one person he trusted most in life.

She answered on the second ring.

"Fi," he said. "I think I'm in trouble again."

FOR SEAN, Lakota's own dead-of-night call hadn't bothered him. He'd been sitting in his TV room, staring at screen static for the past... Hell, he hadn't known how long it'd been since the station had gone off the air.

All he'd known was that he couldn't move from his chair. Not after tonight, when Fiona had made it painfully clear that there would never be more than physical intimacy between them.

But he'd been a fool to hope otherwise. She was right. She'd never promised him anything, so why had he expected it?

Because of what was in her eyes.

It seemed so simple, didn't it?

Now, hours later as the sun rose through the window of his office, Sean tried to get his mind back on work yet again, because this was urgent. No time for messing around, agonizing over something he couldn't have.

He needed his job to save him. It had always provided an identity when everything else faded or crashed down around him. It had always been there for him, even during the downhill ride of the past few years.

Only now, when he had nothing else, did he realize how much his profession should've meant to him.

His assistant, Carly, rushed into the office, her hair in a still-wet-from-the-shower ponytail. He'd gotten the poor girl out of bed, enlisting her help in the mess Lakota had helped to create.

"I've got them," she said, holding up a manila envelope like it was the Olympic torch.

"You miracle worker," said Sean, in full business mode. Here it went: the pressure, the image voodoo.

"I have to tell you," said the girl, handing over the materials, "your phone calls to the right people helped. I only hope copies weren't made."

Sean opened the envelope, slipped out the contents.

One videotape. One packet of negatives and pictures, recently developed at an all-night photo shop. Dohenny's people had sold them for a hefty price, claiming that one more kiss with a pretty girl wouldn't do the actor any harm or any good, either way.

"You can bet someone has insurance with the video," he said. "I talked to The Cool Cat Lounge, as well as Conrad Dohenny's publicist. They're all happy to keep this under wraps, especially since our big box-office star looks like an asshole on the tape."

"But he's so cute," said Carly.

He held up a warning finger. "Don't ever date anyone in the biz."

When she grinned, Sean knew his advice was useless. He sifted through the pictures, coming upon the one where Conrad was sticking his tongue down Lakota's throat. This could come in handy.

"Thanks, Carly," he said. "I owe you big time."

The assistant nodded and left the office.

Sean flapped the picture against the desk. Had Fiona managed to get a hold of anything? How was she doing on her end?

Hell, why worry. She didn't want anything to do with him, so why should he be concerned about helping her out?

The picture caught his attention again. Lakota looked like she wasn't fighting Dohenny, even though she'd said she hadn't meant for things to go this far. Connecting her with a superstar would do wonders for her career. She could ride the story's coattails to something bigger.

If he could manage to spin the story into something more than it was, he could build her up.

Sure, Linc would look like a cuckold, and that would put the clamps on Fiona to spin it the other way. Bottom line: this picture could hurt them both.

So should he use it for Lakota's advantage?

He paused only for a second, then picked up the phone.

MAC HAD ASKED her to meet him in the office's conference room, but that hadn't stopped Louis Martin from butting in on them.

She'd managed to get a copy of the tape—an inferior one, she thought, watching the original that Mac had procured—but that was all she'd secured.

However, it was all she needed, unless more copies of the tape existed.

The three of them watched the events unfold on a television screen. Fiona struggled to keep her mind on the analysis, having been successful at treating Mac as a business associate so far.

Personal concerns had no place right now.

Last night's Cool Cat fiasco played out before them: Linc and Lakota's melancholy exchange, Dohenny's attack, the fire.

By the time the show ended, their boss had already jumped out of his chair. "This is the best thing that could've happened."

Fiona thought about Linc's woeful phone call, his crushed heart. Lakota's ambition and jealousy. "How does a fire translate into 'good'?"

Louis rubbed his hands together, eyes focused on the ceiling. "Don't be so softhearted, Cruz. Mr. Dohenny's going to pay for the fire damage. It was smart of you to suggest assault charges as leverage since the tape clearly shows who's at fault."

Fiona clutched the arms of her chair. "This tape makes Linc look like a bar brawler."

She caught Mac stroking his stubble at the other end of the table, and her skin heated.

Louis gestured toward the TV. "This is your chance to give Lincoln Castle a personality. You can get a lot of mileage out of an alpha-male type. Women swoon for that stuff."

The boss turned to Mac, seeking agreement, but without even looking, Fiona knew Mac wouldn't acknowledge Louis.

"Anyway," he continued, "you guys can really play it up. If the tape just happens to get leaked to the press, you can spin it as Lincoln Castle defending his lady love from a rapacious brat *and* a fire. Lakota will bask in a lot of press, too, if you get it right. This is a publicist's paradise."

Memories assaulted her: Her last job, a golden opportunity, a massive blowout resulting in her shame.

Nothing was foolproof.

Louis shuffled toward the door. "We'll see your true colors, my worker bees."

Mac's chair moaned as he leaned back his head, apparently trying his best to ignore Louis. The slight worked, because their boss's face flamed.

"Don't assume that arrogance, McIntyre. Straight

up, your job is on the line. In fact,'' he darted a glance at Fiona, ''let's just say there's going to be a few less jobs at the end of the month. Layoffs, unfortunately. And there'll probably be room for only one of you.''

Fiona shot up in her chair, driven by fear. ''Is that some kind of threat?''

''It's reality.'' Louis opened the door. ''I'd say 'May the best man win,' but Cruz hasn't proven that she's got any balls yet. And that's a disappointment.''

On that note, he left. Left Fiona feeling sapped, mortified. Before getting fired from her last job, no one would've talked to her with such derision. Back then, she'd been flying high, only to crash and burn in the next minute. Without warning.

She chanced a look at Mac. He was staring at the table, jaw gritted so tightly she thought his head would smash into pieces. But it seemed as if something had imploded inside him already.

''If you're anything like me,'' he said, tone riding a blade of anger, ''you're ready to shove this table down Martie's throat.''

Could they talk to each other without all their personal anguish coming to the surface? Could they keep their love lives out of the office, as promised?

''I'd like nothing better than to feed him some desk.'' Fiona watched him, almost wishing he'd make eye contact, even if she didn't deserve it. ''He's been Big Brothering me since day one.''

''Why does it matter?'' asked Mac, finally looking up. ''What happened at your last firm?''

As soon as their gazes locked, Fiona was a goner,

lost in his eyes, the wounded loneliness, the wary caution.

Maybe, just this once, she could offer a part of herself to him. If it was a consolation prize, then so be it, but at least it was something she could give him without losing her entire sense of self.

"I dropped the ball," she said, smiling to ease the burden.

"You?"

"Yeah." She swallowed, coating her scratchy throat. "Me. I represented Candy-O."

"Wow. Big-time punk actress," said Mac, duly impressed. His admiration fortified her, even temporarily.

"Even after what I did, yes, she is. I thought I'd reached the heights of my career by getting Zap Soda to sign her for a series of commercials."

This was sounding more familiar to Sean. As he recalled, Zap Soda and Candy-O had suffered some kind of hush-hush falling-out. "Let me guess. Things blew up in your face."

"Did they ever. It was revealed that Zap's factories were dumping toxic materials into bays, that they were responsible for a lot of wildlife disasters."

"And Candy-O, being the big environmentalist..."

"...freaked out. How could I have made such a misjudgment?" she said. "I'd almost ruined her career by aligning her with evil."

"She's not a forgiving woman, I hear. The toughest businesswoman out there."

"It's the truth."

Sean hadn't thought it possible, but Fiona had

drawn into herself, fading into the cushions of her chair, losing her zest. His father, all over again. If he could have, he would've gone to her, offered her the comfort of his arms.

But he knew how that would turn out. "You could've spun her out of the situation."

"That's what I said. But, instead, she decided to take the error personally, to drum me out of my job." She smiled, probably to cover the embarrassment. "Luckily she kept the debacle under public wraps, so she does have some pity in her soul."

Did she feel the same way about her career as he used to? Did a part of her die every time failure reared its head?

If he knew Fiona, the answer was yes.

Without preamble, she stood, came toward him. Sean's heartbeat went into overdrive as she came closer, then sat in the next seat. He could smell her fresh hair, her skin.

Remnants of his perfume.

"We can't work as a team from across the room like that."

The revelation of her failure had worn her down, replacing his vibrant Fiona with a crinkled copy. It didn't sit well with Sean. He ached to build her up again.

But she wouldn't accept his affection. And he couldn't accept seeing her so sad.

He reached into the envelope, slid the picture of Lakota and Conrad Dohenny down the table in front of her.

"The reason for the Cool Cat scuffle," he said.

She took a good gander at it. "Oh, poor Linc. Does Lakota know you have this?"

"No. It could do wonderful things for her career."

"That's right." Fiona caught his gaze, eyes dark, deep with emotion. "And it would kill Linc to have this plastered all over the papers."

He couldn't do this anymore. Playing with people's lives. Taking orders from a power-monger like Louis. Sitting this close to Fiona and not being able to do anything about it.

She was still wearing her corporate demeanor, but as he watched her, she changed. Softened under his gaze. Her eyes begged for him to stay in this meaningless, empty groove where they could talk around the core matter.

"I can't sit here pretending like I'm not chipping away every time you look at me, Fiona," he whispered.

"Please, don't." Her voice weakened, pleaded.

He leaned his elbows on the table, trying to get her to glance his way, just one more time. "Why are you so damned stubborn? This could be easy, if you'd..."

His words trailed off as a sheet of hair fell forward, covering her face.

"I don't want to deal with this." She laid a finger on Lakota's picture, indicating heartache. Deception.

"Or this," she added.

She pointed to her heart.

He sucked in a breath, tucked her hair behind an

ear. A tear slipped down her face and, with a resigned movement, she snuffed it away with an index finger.

This wasn't what he wanted, seeing her fall apart. It reminded him of coming home to see his dad flake away day by day.

Lakota's picture caught his gaze. Damn games. He'd grown to hate his job, just as much as he hated himself most times.

Truthfully, until Fiona had shown up, he'd despised coming into the office. Despised the fact that he didn't have the strength to leave the predictable routine of his job—his echoing life—behind.

He indicated the photo while getting to his feet. "There's a price to pay for every decision. If that picture leaks to the press, she becomes a tabloid star. Linc looks like a fool. If it's kept in the vault with the negatives…" He left it up to her imagination.

"And what about the security video?" She was peeking up at him, her position inferior to his. For once she wasn't making sure he knew how tough she was.

Impulsively, he moved closer, but Fiona didn't flinch. His heart swelled, making him whole. With slow care, he stroked her hair. She relaxed into his hand, and an eternal moment passed, creating a bubble where nothing else could touch them.

Carly shouted, "Bye, Sean," as she passed in the hallway. The interruption jerked his hand, and Fiona leaned away.

"What do you want to do with the video?" he asked, unable to let go, even if the connection only consisted of his eyes caressing her.

She stared at the table, miles from the old, brusque, it's-all-about-a-good-time Fiona. Sean held his breath.

"I'd just as soon cover that video with a hill of dirt," she said. "The whole episode doesn't sit well with Linc. Or with Lakota, I'll guess."

"Then you've got your answer." He ran his hand over her jaw. One final touch. "Screw Louis and his ambition."

She met his gaze. "Screw our jobs, too, I suppose. He won't be happy."

Who cared about the job part. Or Louis. Living life under the thumb of a creep like Martin wasn't the way to go. It'd taken Fiona to shake Sean up, to awaken him.

He leaned against the table, relieved now that everything seemed so clear.

There was no way he'd stay at Stellar, not after Louis's threat. Not if it'd cost Fiona more than he was willing to pay.

Everything seemed so much simpler now.

Why couldn't she see that, too?

"Don't worry," he said. "We'll take a few hours to find a way to get Linc and Lakota on top."

And then he'd be done, leaving Fiona in peace. Finding some for himself, also.

She smiled at him, a glint of respect underlying all the other emotions he saw in her eyes.

He hoped she wasn't looking too closely, discovering that deep inside, he'd already left the building.

Left *her* because there was no other choice if he wanted to stay in one piece.

14

WHEN LAKOTA ARRIVED at Fiona's World War II-era high-rise apartment across from The Grove shopping center, Linc answered the door.

He was dressed in lounge gear: surf shorts, a Rob Machado T-shirt, his sandy hair sticking up as if he'd been tearing at it.

No greeting. Just a cautious, sweeping glance. They hadn't seen each other since The Cool Cat, and he'd spent the night at his place, shutting her out.

And she knew why. Because of his movie audition and what she'd said to him about being jealous. About keeping him behind in his career.

Linc retreated into the apartment while the aroma of Lobster Bisque filled the air. Fiona's voice accompanied the scent. "Hey, Lakota."

"Hi." She took a look around before going to the cooking alcove. The spin doctor didn't really have much furniture on hand. It was almost like she hadn't bothered to move all the way in. Boxes were stowed under a rickety metal dining table. A futon, beanbag and lawn chair were the only places to sit.

The sight made Lakota a little sad for Fiona, but she wasn't sure exactly why.

When she saw the kitchen, she was struck by the same pity. No oven warmers to add a homey touch, not even a toaster or blender.

Fiona was holding a pair of prongs over a pot of boiling water, steam lending her cheeks a pink-tinged warmth. And she needed it, because the rest of her was downright maudlin, her black hair tied at the nape of her neck, her shorts and top basic and ordinary.

Where had her flair gone?

"You a cook?" Lakota asked to break the ice.

In response, Fiona leaned over, opened the freezer. Packages of single-portion frozen gourmet dinners slumped over each other.

Again, a twinge of sympathy attacked Lakota.

But who was she to feel sorry for someone else? She'd spent a sleepless night, calling Linc's number, not calling it, bothering Sean instead.

Fiona removed a packet of goopy beige matter from the hot water. "You already caught up with Sean?"

"I did." Not that she was happy about her publicist quitting his job today, but he'd told her to stick with Fiona. He sounded so confident in his associate's abilities that Lakota decided that giving her a chance wouldn't be a bad thing.

"Then you're up to speed," said Fiona. "Why don't you take a seat? I'll be out there to talk turkey in a sec."

Maybe that's why the PR rep looked so glum, because she had to handle both Linc and Lakota now. But Lakota was surprised Fiona didn't seem more stressed out by the prospect. Didn't she realize Sean had left all of them behind?

Not that Lakota understood his motivations, she thought, as she wandered to where Linc had plopped onto the futon. Her ex-publicist didn't want to talk about his reasons for quitting; he'd just wanted to reassure her that she'd be well taken care of with Fiona.

Should she sit next to Linc, pretending she hadn't let her ambition get the best of her last night?

Lakota lowered herself to the beanbag, offering a smile to him. "How are you?"

Fiona banged around in the kitchen, bowls clattering together, spoons chirping, providing a background for Linc's frown.

"I miss you," he said.

"Linc." Why'd he have to be so sincere? So open? "How can you say that after what I did?"

"You didn't mean it."

Didn't she? Last night, Conrad Dohenny had seemed like her ticket out of soaps. This morning, she knew she'd been persuaded by champagne, knew that the box-office giant had been full of hot air.

And that Linc was the real thing. "I thought I'd done some maturing after we broke up, you know. But the old Lakota, the one who threw things and had temper tantrums, came back full force last night. She was just more subtle about it."

He held out his arm, and she came to him, resting her head on his shoulder. Ah, there. This was where she was meant to be.

"Maybe I'm just a sucker," he said, "but I love

you too much to let you go. It took me one bout with insomnia to think it over, and the bed felt awful empty without you in it.''

She wrapped her arms around him, sighed, holding him tightly. He enveloped her in his strong arms, and she knew she'd never been so safe in all her life.

He'd never leave her behind.

''That's what I want to see,'' said Fiona, balancing bowls of soup and setting them on a scratched glass coffee table with an unrolled Sunday *L.A. Times* lying on the surface.

She collapsed in the lawn chair, shoulders curled forward instead of thrown back. ''I called you both over for a serious talk. Today's a slow news day, so that's why you haven't seen The Cool Cat video on the air.''

''I hope we don't,'' said Linc, his voice vibrating through Lakota's body.

She held him closer, wondering if Fiona would bring up that Conrad Dohenny kiss picture. It had cost her a pretty penny to buy the thing, but during his last call, Sean said Fiona had possession of it now.

True to the rumor, the publicist produced the photo from under the newspaper, holding it out to Linc and Lakota. The bisque went untouched as they peered at Conrad and his invasive tongue.

After a moment, Linc tossed it away. Lakota watched it arc through the air and jet to a graceful landing on the shag carpet.

Fiona ignored Linc's cavalier gesture. ''Lakota, do you want the tape released?''

Though the memory of Linc defending her some-what appealed, she didn't want to come off as a help-less weakling who stood in corners while men rescued her. That didn't mesh with the action heroine prime-time plans. "No."

"How about the picture?"

Linc's arms stiffened, and she knew it was because he was reliving Conrad's tongue in her mouth. She wished she could forget his stale-alcohol taste, the wet, sloppy, drunken celebrity spit.

When Lakota didn't say anything, Fiona continued. "PR wise, it would give you exposure. But is it the kind of reputation you want?"

Conrad's New Whore! She could see the headlines, could imagine the interviews on the tabloid TV shows, could almost digest the offers: *Playboy, Penthouse,* maybe a cheesy reality television hostessing job.

And Linc. What would the publicity do to him? It would make him seem stomped-on, cast-off.

For Lakota, the picture lost its colors right before her eyes.

"There's a lot more to you than kissing Conrad," said Fiona. "And I'm not really sounding as ambitious as a real PR rep, am I?" She laughed, but without mirth.

"Thank you," said Lakota. "But I'd rather keep a little dignity. What I have of it."

Linc blew out a breath. "Thank God."

"I'm never letting you down again," said Lakota, pressing her cheek against a chest made for her.

"Excellent." Fiona clapped her hands together, minus the enthusiasm.

Where had the tiger gone?

"So," the publicist continued, "Sean and I talked about several ways to market the two of you. Fairytale couple. Linc and his own photographs, showing the deep, sensitive artist he is. If that Roger Reiking movie happens, we'll need to step up the pub."

"It'll happen," said Lakota, sending a worshipful gaze up at him.

He kissed her forehead, smiled against her skin. "And Lakota?"

"We could explore avenues for her love of vintage items." Fiona poked at her bisque with a spoon. "A show on the Travel Network, for instance, where she can spotlight different antique malls across the country. Or maybe you could mix that with adventurous trips, to project that image, I mean. Sean couldn't make it here tonight, but we'll brainstorm with him later. We just wanted to ask you both about the picture and video before we acted."

What was she talking about? "Fiona, I don't think Sean's going to want anything to do with this."

The other woman gave Lakota a confused glance. "He'd better."

"Why? He quit so he doesn't have to deal with other people's baggage anymore. At least, that's what he told me an hour ago."

Fiona just sat there with her mouth open. Linc, however, spoke for her.

"Kota, you must've misunderstood him."

''No, he was clear.''

Fiona darted up from her lawn chair, started pacing. ''I can't believe this,'' she said to no one in particular. ''I knew he was pissed at Louis, but... What exactly did he say?''

So he *hadn't* told Fiona. Weird. ''Um, maybe you two had better talk. Don't you think?''

Linc nodded sagely. ''Fi, when you told me you and McIntyre were almost finished...personally... Does this have anything to do with that?''

''I don't know.'' She stopped fidgeting, and some of the liveliness flushed back into her cheeks. ''He can't do this. Not when he's so damned good.''

''I guess I owe you a kiss for that bet,'' said Lakota to Linc. ''She chased my publicist away from his work, she's such a heartbreaker.''

Linc leaned his mouth toward her ear. ''Later.''

Oh, yeah, there'd be a ''later.'' She'd make sure ''later'' made up for all her shortcomings.

Louder, Linc said, ''Call him, Fi.''

''Oh.'' Her eyes widened, and her hands flew in front of her chest, barring the suggestion. ''He won't want to talk with me.''

Linc whipped out his cell phone. ''Kota, what's his number?''

She flashed out her own device, pressed speed dial, handed it to Fiona.

''No,'' the woman said. Boy, did she look horrified.

''It's ringing,'' said Lakota.

Fiona frowned, fluttered her hands—yeah, *fluttered*—and finally grabbed the phone, retreating down the hallway. A door closed, and Lakota cuddled up to Linc again.

"It's time for me to pay up," she said, voice sultry and very Rita Wilde-ish.

"I think the bet's a draw," he said, adjusting her so her mouth was near his, her heart pulsing against his chest. "They're both losers until they work this out."

"We're not. I'm going to take you higher than the clouds, and never let you down."

Linc laughed, rubbed his lips against hers. His words were soft kisses, hinting, promising. "Wasn't that from Script 1024? Rita and Colt Rettinger's first kiss?"

Lakota felt herself blushing. "So sue me if I'm a little tongue-tied. I can't think when you're around."

"Then don't think."

His mouth met hers, warm, inviting, all-encompassing. Her senses whirled with the musky scent of his skin, the soap he used every morning, the scratch and burn of emerging whiskers, the sound of them tasting each other.

Minutes must have passed, all of them filled with nothing but dizziness and contentment, a nap on a sandy beach under the sun with waves singing her to sleep. The next thing she knew, Fiona was back in the room, setting Lakota's phone next to the uneaten soup. The woman couldn't keep the longing from her eyes, her posture.

Lakota and Linc still touched each other, smiling at Fiona.

"I guess you've proven me wrong," said the PR woman.

"Finally?" asked Linc, fondness carrying his voice.

"Finally." She'd dropped her facade and, in its place, stood a revealed woman, stripped of protection. "You two show me that maybe things can work."

She closed her eyes, then opened them, exposing a place so vulnerable, even Lakota gasped.

"He's coming over," said Fiona, a quiver in her tone. "To my place."

WHEN FIONA had gotten the news about Sean quitting, she finally understood the definition of loneliness. Of hurt.

After their time in the office today, she'd expected to see him tomorrow, and the day after that. But she wouldn't anymore. The realization left her flailing for an emotional handle. She hadn't wanted to admit it, but she was in love with the guy.

In love.

Oh, God. What if he turned out to be another Ted? What if he used her up and tossed her away after he'd gotten tired of her? How would she cope?

Could she?

The strange thing was, it'd actually wound her more to never see Sean again, wouldn't it? Yet maybe being with him was worth all the pain, all the numbness of being rejected.

What if...?

Fiona almost didn't dare wonder, but couldn't stop herself.

What if Sean really did love her, too?

As she waited for him to knock at 11:00 p.m. on the Sunday night before the bet expired, Fiona tried not to bite her lip in a fit of nerves. She'd ruin the makeup she'd put on because she wanted to impress him. She'd even taken a yellow dress out from the back of her closet, something she hadn't worn since… Well, since she'd believed in soap-bubble dreams.

When she'd last been in love.

Yup, this was actually her. Fiona Cruz. Totally out of control.

Totally on the line.

When the knock came, it startled her, even if she'd been expecting it. She walked to the door, and every barefooted step seemed like a tour through a dream—surreal, unmanageable.

She opened the door to find Sean, worse for the wear, his white shirt uneven because he'd lined up the buttons incorrectly and slipped them through the wrong holes. His dark-blond hair kicked up in places, stubborn as the man himself, his green eyes sharp and broken as discarded glass littering a gutted-out street. Even his outlaw-careless smile had lost its edge.

She'd never been so damned glad to see anyone.

"You quit, did you?" she asked, holding on to the door frame for support. They hadn't talked about this over the phone. It'd been hard enough to invite him over.

Because Fiona *never* allowed men in.

He was busy scanning her, the hunger in his gaze

almost scratching at her. ''I didn't want to distract you with my drama. I... Is that what this is about?''

Definitely not.

She flew at him, taking a fistful of shirt in hand, pulling him toward her until they were kissing, almost swallowing each other up in their desperate good-to-see-you-again.

His hands were planted in her hair, angling her head, positioning her so his mouth could devour. Her arms hooked upward, clinging, fingers abrading his hunched-over back.

They swayed together, stealing each other's air, pressing, urging, seeking.

Fiona's heart was near to bursting with happiness, the culmination of all that wanting and waiting.

As they back-stepped into her apartment, he kicked the door closed, then slowed down the pace, sliding a thumb under her chin, petting her neck, stretching the kiss into one long marathon of moaning desire.

Fiona hadn't kissed like this since she was a teenager, exploring, half-afraid of what might come next. That same innocence captured her now, and a laugh bubbled in her chest because she was so thankful for the return of it.

Oh, it was good to relax, to be held up by his strong arms, to know he wouldn't let her fall just because her knees were turning to orange marmalade. There was no need to wrestle him, to let her body tell him that she had just as much power—if not more—than he did.

No, this was different, like nothing she'd ever felt

before. Lazy, sweeping pulses of the lips, a sipping sweetness that allowed her time to open her eyes half-way, to spy on him through her lashes, to stroke along with every slow glide of his mouth, to sample the mint of the gum he'd probably been chewing before knocking on her door.

Cocky bastard.

He'd maneuvered her through the living room, past the skeletons of her furniture and her old life, toward the bedroom. She let him guide her farther, willing to go wherever he'd take her.

"You never gave me an explanation—" she gasped as he tenderly kissed her earlobe "—Sean."

He paused, long enough for her to hear their blood echoing in each other's veins. "Sean. I like the way it sounds when you say it."

They stopped in a slant of moonlight coming through her window; it reclined on her bed, the centerpiece of yet another room she needed to lend some life to.

"Why did you leave today and not even tell me?" she asked, smoothing her knuckles over a cheekbone. This time, she didn't have to pretend she wasn't feeling anything.

He smiled, and Fiona framed his face with her hands. A work of imperfect art.

"I realized," he said, "that I was sticking around for the wrong reasons. Life is too short to spend it pleasing people like Louis, living the lives of others when I didn't have one myself. And I left because you wanted the job more than I did."

"Oh, Sean."

Should she say it? The L-word? He'd just admitted that he'd made a sacrifice because of her. The words built up in a ball of anxiety yet, still, Fiona hesitated.

He stepped forward, and the moonlight highlighted her lipstick on his cheek.

Marked territory. Hers.

This time, she left the brand alone.

"I love you," she said.

She never been so vulnerable in all her life.

A pent-up breath shuddered out of her, as she added, "I love you so much that it might be the end of me."

She laughed at the exaggeration, knowing it was true, anyway.

"Stop that." He traced a finger under her jawline, drawing her gaze to his.

Every splinter of color in his green eyes revealed a different path into the future. A future with him.

"I love you, too, Fiona. I have for a while."

Thank God. "I'm scared." There, she'd finally said *that,* too. Her shoulders relaxed, the weight lifted off of them. "I'm so afraid of what might happen, because…"

"What?" he asked gently.

She smiled, tilting her head at him to control the weariness. But then, tired of holding it in, she let it go with a tiny, sad laugh. "I was engaged once."

He squeezed her bare shoulder, stopping the imminent flow of tears. "A disappointment from the past."

"Right." Now he was using his fingertips to lull

her, dragging them over her collarbone. She moved with drowsy, sexy caresses. So much better, so much... "He fell in love with my best friend, and they went on to have a baby, a nice house, a cozy marriage. I couldn't have given that to him, you know? I've lived with that knowledge for years, proving myself right, I guess."

His fingers eased behind her neck, kneading the tightened muscles, causing jagged bolts of warmth to steal through her.

"It's so much easier to disappoint yourself rather than having someone else do it for you," she said.

"You don't ever need to worry about that again."

He stole his fingers under one of her dress straps. His touch heated onto the patch of skin that had so recently been covered. It made her suck in a gust of air.

She recovered, shrugging so that the strap tumbled down one shoulder. "We did things a little backward, didn't we? First comes sex, then comes love... I'm not sure what comes after that."

"Marriage?" The word came out thick, heavy.

"It won't be like it was with your dad," she said, taking his hands and tugging him toward the bed. She wanted him so badly she was about to combust.

"I'm willing to take that leap of faith," he said. "As long as I've got you jumping with me."

She turned around, tacitly asking him to undo her dress. He did, the zipper groaning down in its descent, the night air shivering her skin as the folds of material parted, opened.

As she stepped out of the clothing, Sean took off his shirt, his pants.

No underwear for him though.

He moved toward her, hitched his thumbs over the elastic of her comfy briefs. Tugging, he let the air breathe over her, then pulled them all the way off.

She braced herself on one of his shoulders—something she'd be free to do from now on if she needed it—while she stepped out of the undies.

Then, in a slow journey, he ran his hands over her body, memorizing the shape of her arms, her plump breasts, her rib cage, the swerve of her waist, her belly. She saw herself through his eyes: a woman's woman, with extra curves here and there, with voluptuous promises to offer the right man.

She saw everything now.

And, as he looked into her eyes, she knew he saw, too.

A glance at the clock by her bed revealed that it was 11:59. One minute before the bet was supposed to end.

Oddly enough, she didn't really mind losing this time.

Fiona kissed her prize again, flowing into him, taking him back with her until they could crawl onto the bed. Her body fit perfectly beneath his, ready to be orchestrated, played by his hands. His mouth.

He teased her breasts to hard peaks with his fingers, licking her nipple, blowing on it until she thought she'd cry out from the sharp sensation. Drowning in pleasure, she skimmed her toes over his calf, between his legs, up, up, until she reached his inner thighs, then down.

Nice, this leisurely exploration of each other. She took her time learning every thatch of fine hair on his chest, sifting through it with her distended nipples until the wisp of skin on skin made her wiggle her hips, slipping over his rigid penis with the slickness of her growing excitement.

She'd grown swollen with wanting him, blood pounding between her legs, making her ache, stiffen, search him out.

He used his fingers to work her further along, his thumb circling her clit, awakening a rhythm in her hips that corresponded to every stroke. When he nestled two fingers inside her, slipping in and out with fluid thrusts, she grabbed at his arms, needing to be anchored before she took off.

He pushed her until she thought she would shatter. But she held on, moaning, louder, louder, until she hung halfway off the bed, her hair brushing the carpet, her torso arched, her sex rocking against his hand.

"Fiona," he growled, as if she was getting away.

With one tug of his arms, she was back on the bed, beads of sweat dripping down her skin as she sat upright. She positioned herself against the pillows, one leg still off the bed.

While she panted, he left her for a second.

"Get back here," she said, laughing, ecstatic. So giddy and full of electricity. "I'm not done with you."

He prowled back to her, a predator. "One last layer of protection, Fi, and you're mine."

Rubber. She felt it covering his hard-on as he coasted along her inner thigh, as she spread herself open for him and thrust her hips up to take him inside.

They strained together, sweat mingling, muscles laboring. With smooth strokes, he pounded into her, and she gyrated her hips, wanting more. Getting more.

The cadence of their lovemaking increased, with him ramming forward. She accepted every drive, every bolt of collecting heat that was gathering in her core, flaming upward, tearing through her belly, her limbs.

Everywhere.

He consumed her, covering her, lending her breath as he kissed her to climax. Lightning, swift as the bite of a night creature, flashed into her body, her brain, illuminating her from the inside out.

Ripping her apart. Zinging her back together again.

Washing her in perspiration as a fall of soft contentment pattered her back to reality. One final rumble of thunder roared through her body as she bucked against him.

He hadn't spent himself yet, and she reached between his legs from the back, finding a place she knew would give him release.

Laboring, groaning, releasing, he shuddered from the same storm, collapsing against her.

This time, when it was over, they lingered, holding each other.

That lipstick was still on his cheek. "You've got something," she said, flicking a finger over the mark.

At first, he didn't seem to get it. Then a smile beamed over his face.

"It's there to stay," he said. "Branded."

She snuggled into him and, for the first time since…well, never…she fell asleep in a man's arms, in her own bed.

Dreaming of paradise.

Epilogue

ON A WHITE-SAND BEACH in St. Vincent, pristine mosquito netting rode a tropical breeze. The material was attached to a gazebo, the pale structure contrasting with the gem-blue of the sea and the lush vegetation.

Everything was more vivid out here, Sean thought as he tipped back an ice-flaked bottle of beer. More alive.

Just as he'd been these past two months.

The netting parted, letting in the sun. The light flashed off the band of gold on his finger, the ring winking at him.

He tossed away the magazine he'd been reading. *People*, complete with an article about Lincoln Castle, and how he'd become a hero by saving a drowning child while the actor was on location in Europe for that romantic comedy.

Linc's new publicist was good. He had to hand that to her. She'd also gotten Lakota good exposure for a valuable painting she'd discovered in one of those vintage stores.

A silhouette blocked the sun, shading him. A figure as voluptuous as the local fruit he'd been eating lately.

She moved forward. Fiona. His wife.

The sun filtered over her, and he saw that she balanced a fruit platter in her hands. Bananas, coconuts, oranges and...

He laughed. A spray of maraschino cherries.

"*People* magazine, huh?" She sat next to him, plucked a cherry from the selection of snacks. "My former assistant has really been good for Linc."

"Rosie's been good for Lakota, also." As she ran the cherry over his bare chest, his nipples tightened. Tease.

"Where Linc goes, so does Lakota. You talked to her last. Isn't she due back on the soap next week?"

Lakota was working on that travel show Fiona had suggested before she quit Stellar. Still going to auditions, still hanging in there.

"Let's talk about something else," he said. "Namely..."

He pulled her into his arms, hugging her until she nuzzled against his neck. "...not talking."

"Okay," Fiona mouthed, sighing into her cozy spot.

He enjoyed the feel of her, would for the rest of his life. Even if they were interrupting their jaunt around the Caribbean—on both their tabs, even if he had technically won the bet—they'd always be on a holiday. Next week, they'd be returning to the States to meet his family, her family, to see Linc and Lakota, who were a lot like family.

After that they could go wherever they pleased, until their comfortable savings ran out. Then...? They'd talked about opening a bar on the sands of some island maybe, living real lives and not existing through others.

"Sorry to break the silence…" she said, sketching her fingers over his legs, higher…

"No you're not."

She laughed. "…but I brought reading material, too."

She produced a book from the folds of her sarong. *The Sensuous Woman.*

"Think I can practice The Butterfly Flick?" she asked, all playfulness.

The Flick. They hadn't gotten around to actually doing it until things had been worked out between them, once and for all.

It'd been worth the wait.

"Anything for literacy," he said, sinking down in his lounge chair as Fiona undid the drawstring on his pants. "Anything to keep you happy."

And as that wolfish howl returned and screamed through his veins once again, he knew it cried for only one person.

Fiona. And it always would.

He'd bet on it.

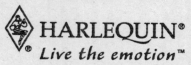

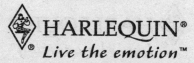

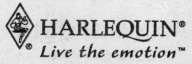

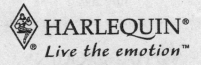

HARLEQUIN®

Temptation

THE WRONG BED

What happens when a girl finds herself in the *wrong* bed...with the *right* guy?

Find out in:

#866 NAUGHTY BY NATURE by Jule McBride
February 2002

#870 SOMETHING WILD by Toni Blake
March 2002

#874 CARRIED AWAY by Donna Kauffman
April 2002

#878 HER PERFECT STRANGER by Jill Shalvis
May 2002

#882 BARELY MISTAKEN by Jennifer LaBrecque
June 2002

#886 TWO TO TANGLE by Leslie Kelly
July 2002

Midnight mix-ups have never been so much fun!

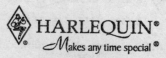

HARLEQUIN®
Makes any time special ®

Visit us at www.eHarlequin.com

HTNBN2